UPRISING

After the accidental defeat of General Gerasimov and his army by The Red Neval spaceship, crowds of people gather to see the spectacle and rummage around in the ruins and carnage for souvenirs. Smoke billows high in the sky and The Red Neval burns white hot and displays a fascinating interior to an anxious, inquisitive crowd. Reports of an alien invasion are now being broadcast across the airwaves and talk of goblins, ghouls and doppelgangers spread throughout the city like butter on a hot knife. Some residence are getting ready to evacuate, whilst others take to the streets in search of the alien invaders. Armed with screwdrivers and pitch forks they scurry down the streets like logs caught in a flood, shouting out, 'Death to the goblin monsters, kill them all!'. Buildings burn, businesses lay crumbled and ruined and the annual Vodka and Soft Drink Autumn Festival is definitely over.

ACT 1, SCENE 1

1.57pm. Saturday 18th October, 2025, The Red Square, Moscow. Dmitry, Yuri, London and his team of ex-SAS soldiers, the alien MacTavish and the kinetic based life-form, KAL, have taken cover in a clothes and handbag shop. Inside the shop, they find the Moon Man prancing around in the store wearing a shiny new orange outfit. Outside on the streets, an angry, hungry mob, led by Miss Decapinovsky search for Dmitry and Yuri and the others, believing them to be Goblins from another planet who have taken on human form.

MISS DECAPINOVSKY
Keep looking for them, they must be around here somewhere...

> (Miss Decapinovsky turns over
> a bin and some rats scurry
> away.)

...Rats. That's it! They must be hiding in one of the shops. We need to double back on ourselves...

> (Miss Decapinovsky turns to
> face her newly formed gang
> and reiterates her words with
> great volume.)

UPRISING

A COMEDY SCI-FI ADVENTURE SERIES

BY

SAM LUCAS

...I am a good pickpocket. The secret is to replace a heavy item with something of similar weight....

BOOK FOUR - PART ONE

OSCAR PISCINE BOOK PUBLISHING

ISBN 978-1-7398855-6-4

Paperback Version

UPRISING: PART ONE BY SAM LUCAS © 2023

WWW.SAMLUCASBOOKS.COM
e-mail:samlucasbooks@btinternet.com

PUBLISHER - OSCAR PISCINE BOOKS

...They must have slipped into one of the shops...

(*The gang mumble and groan like zombies whilst poking and jabbing at inanimate objects that lay in the street.*)

...We will split up. Mrs Plumitry, you take this half and I will take the rest.

(*Miss Decapinovsky points at a plump lady in her 80's wearing a MacIver tartan skirt, red shoes and a white blouse.*)

                MRS PLUMITRY
But I've never led a gang before?

              MISS DECAPINOVSKY
This is no time to lose your spine woman, we are under attack. If we don't act fast we could all end up like those cosmonauts; cabbages pretending to be humans.

                MRS PLUMITRY
Alright, since you put it like that, I'll do it. But I've never really

been fond of cabbage, I'm more of a
carrot and parsnips woman myself.

            MISS DECAPINOVSKY
Good, then that's settled. We'll
meet up back at the Square in fifteen
minutes...

    (The gang split into two
    groups and walk off in
    different directions. Miss
    Decapinovsky and her gang
    walk back towards the street
    where Dmitry, Yuri and the
    rest are hiding. Pilkington
    moves from his crouched
    position behind a counter and
    knocks over a vase. The
    sound of the vase breaking
    echoes out in the street
    alerting the alien hunters.
    Miss Decapinovsky stops in
    her tracks and looks towards
    the clothes shop.)

...come out, come out, wherever you
are, we know you are hiding. It is
only a matter of time before we find
you. If you show yourselves, we will
kill you quick.

    (London moves from behind a
    curtain and looks over
    towards Pilkington
    disapprovingly.)

                    LONDON
That's torn it...

            (London peers out into the
            street and looks at the angry
            mob. They are walking
            towards the shop.)

...They are coming this way!

                    CAVENDISH
How many are there?

                    LONDON
About 30 I would say.

                    CAVENDISH
30? That's a bit much to take on
with coat hangers and handbags. I
say we make a run for it out the
back.

                    LONDON
Make a run for it? Am I hearing you
right Cavendish? I thought you were
a one man army! Sounds a bit
cowardly to run from a load of
civilians armed with screwdrivers and
pitch forks.

                    CAVENDISH
Cowardly? I like a good fight as
much as the next bloke, but I also

like to live to tell the tale. If
you're such a hard man, why don't you
go out there and confront them?

                    LONDON
Have to say, I feel a bit naked
without the old *Webley* to pick a few
off with. I'm quite fond of the old
hand to hand combat stuff, but 30's a
bit much for me these days...

> *(London peers outside from*
> *behind a curtain.)*

...However, there was a time I could
have taken on that many with one arm
tied behind my back...

> *(Outside in the street, an*
> *open manhole cover has*
> *attracted the attention of*
> *Miss Decapinovsky.)*

...Wait a minute! They've stopped.
The woman that seems to be the leader
is checking out an open manhole
cover.

> *(Dmitry and Yuri raise their*
> *heads above the shop counter*
> *and look outside.)*

                    DMITRY
That is Miss Decapinovsky. We have
met her before, she is nuts. She

thinks we are all goblins...

>   (Dmitry looks over to KAL and
>   MacTavish.)

...But our new friends will only
reinforce her misconception. It is
probably best we disassociate
ourselves with these two and throw
them out the front window. While
they are being beaten to death and
getting stabbed by screwdrivers, we
can make our escape out the back
door.

>   (KAL looks across to
>   MacTavish who is busy filling
>   his pockets with bottles of
>   leather cleaner.)

                    KAL
MacTavish?

                    MACTAVISH
Aye.

                    KAL
What have you got there?

                    MACTAVISH
A dinnae ken, bit it's fine. A real

taste o' the liquid gold fae the
highlands o' EgÁs.

                    KAL
They want to kill us!

        (MacTavish's eyes begin to
        close and he is finding it
        hard to stay conscious.)

                  MACTAVISH
Eh!

        (Carter looks outside through
        a crack in the window.)

                   CARTER
I'm with Dmitry. Let's throw them
outside and make a run for it.

                   LONDON
Sshh! They've stopped...

        (London watches Miss
        Decapinovsky go down the
        manhole.)

...That woman you know has gone into
the sewer. They must be thinking
we've gone underground.

                    CARTER
That's not a bad idea, we can go
right across the city undetected. My
grandfather new all about the sewers.
Tosher he was...

        *(Cavendish cuts Carter off in
        mid sentence.)*

                    CAVENDISH
We know, you told us before, but
didn't you say your grandfather died
in the sewer?

                    CARTER
Yeh, but he knew all about them.
That's all I'm saying.

                    LONDON
Quiet, they'll hear us!

        *(MacTavish starts to sing a
        song with the heartiness of a
        drunk at 3am in the morning.)*

                    CARTER
Oi, shut it!...

        (Carter looks across at KAL.)

...Tell your friend to belt up or
I'll sock him in the face.

        (KAL seems to be motionless

and frozen in time.)

...Oi, there's something wrong with this one...

(Carter prods KAL.)

...This one's dead!

> *(They all look. Yuri crawls over the top of Winslow and goes over to KAL and Carter.)*

YURI
Looks like he is dead. Stiff as a board with no pulse.

DMITRY
Did he ever have a pulse?

YURI
I don't know, but he has not got one now.

> *(MacTavish continues to sing.)*

CARTER
That's it, I warned you.

> *(The Moon Man stands up from his crouched position and walks in front of Carter.)*

                    MOON MAN
You leave him be. He hasn't done
anything to you. You're just like
all the rest, violence first.

          (The Moon Man walks over to
          MacTavish and his singing
          gets louder.)

                    CARTER
That's it! I warned you.

                    MOON MAN
Don't you dare...

          (Carter goes to punch
          MacTavish and hits the Moon
          Man by mistake. The Moon Man
          is knocked out and falls on
          top of MacTavish. MacTavish
          continues to sing, but it is
          now successfully muffled.)

                    CAVENDISH
Be quiet, I can hear trucks!

          (London looks down the
          street.)

                    LONDON
You're right Cavendish, two trucks, a
jeep and a motorcycle. They are
coming this way. Looks like top
brass.

CAVENDISH
Do you think we should go now?

LONDON
Under the circumstances, perhaps we
should leave.

*(The army vehicles thunder
down the street at great
speed. Miss Decapinovsky
pokes her head out of the
manhole to find out what the
noise is and the army
vehicles drive by. A
splatter of blood fills the
streets and the trucks come
to a sudden stop. The rest
of her gang run away in
horror.)*

PILKINGTON
Oh, did you see that. That woman has
lost her head.

LONDON
Better hers than ours Pilky. Right,
c'mon everyone, we're getting out of
here...

*(London walks over to Yuri
and Dmitry.)*

LONDON
Right we're off. Hope to catch up at

some point and hear all about how you got off that *Space Station*. Shame we can't take that alien fellow with us, but that's asking for trouble. Well, there's no time for long speeches. See you on the other side.

> *(London and his band of ex-SAS soldiers go to the back off the shop and exit onto the street and run off out of sight down a narrow alley. Inside the shop, Dmitry and Yuri look out into the street and watch as a platoon of soldiers emerge from the back of a truck. From a jeep in front of them, a General climbs out and begins to gesticulate.)*

GENERAL SPURIOVSKY
Search the area, they must be around here somewhere...

> *(General Spuriovsky is a small man and stands only 5ft 2". He walks with a gold cane and favours his left side. He is wearing a white uniform with many medals and a monocle hangs down his chest from a cord, but his most notable feature is a large imperial moustache.)*

YURI

That is General Spuriovsky. Now I
see the face, it is all coming back
to me.

DMITRY

Do you know this guy?

YURI

I have met him a few times before
when I was young. He used to come to
my parents house and meet with my
father. They were always arguing
about a gold artefact of some kind
and an accident that happened in the
town of Dalnegorsk.

DMITRY

Dalnegorsk? That name rings a bell
for some reason, and I am sure I have
heard of him before.

YURI

You have. If you remember, when we
were on truck with Sgt. Smithsky, he
was telling the Corporal that he
wasn't going to contact General
Spuriovsky because it was 'bridge
night'.

DMITRY

Yes, I remember. A lot has happened
since then, but it was only two days
ago.

YURI

I knew I knew the name, but I never
made the connection. My father used
to talk of him with disdain. He is
the reason my father left the army,
but it is very foggy in my brain. I
was just a teenager when I met him.

> *(Yuri and Dmitry hide down
> behind the shop counter.)*

GENERAL SPURIOVSKY

You men take this side of the street
and the others this side. There is a
bottle of 50 year old *Budgie* Vodka to
the person who brings me the heads of
Yuri Chekov and Dmitry Usakov...

> *(The soldiers all cheer with
> joy. The General then pulls
> out a golden ticket.)*

...And a season pass for the Pripyat
Amusement Park for anyone who finds
the aliens that arrived in that
ship...

> *(The soldiers cheer even
> louder.)*

...Now, go find them.

> *(The soldiers split up into
> groups of two and start to
> search the shops.)*

DMITRY

Stupid soldiers. They don't even know what they are going to win and our heads are at stake. The Pripyat Amusement Park closed in 1986 and is heavily contaminated with radiation.

YURI

And who would want a 50 year old bottle of *Budgie* vodka.

DMITRY

I thought they had banned that stuff?

YURI

They did. The humane society fought for an injunction against production of drink after it was discovered they put thousands of dead birds into vat to help with the fermentation process.

(Dmitry looks above the counter.)

DMITRY

I think they are coming in here. We better leave now.

YURI

What about Moon Man and the aliens?

                    DMITRY
What good are they to us? A broken
robot, a drunken idiot who sounds
like a parrot when he speaks and a
large carrot with a traffic cone on
his head. Leave them here. We have
enough problems of our own.

                    YURI
Where will we go?

                    DMITRY
I don't know, but anywhere is better
than here.

        *(Dmitry and Yuri exit the
        shop through the back door
        and run down the street.)*

Scene fades.

ACT 1, SCENE 2

8.32am, 30th January 1986, Dalnegorsk,
Russia.   Colonel P. Chekov is in
command of a small unit sent to
investigate the possible crash landing
of a U.F.O into the side of Mount
Izvestkovaya. The unit fly in on a
MI-24 helicopter and land by a black
gravel road covered with patches of
ice and snow. At first glance they
see nothing unusual and set up a base
camp and make preparations for lunch.
At 10.36am, troops are sent out to
search the mountainside and look for
the downed craft. After a search of
only 8 minutes, a strange unearthly
figure is found lying in the snow - it
is still alive!

SOLDIER 1
Here! Look, I have found an alien.
It's still alive!

SOLDIER 2
I'll get the Colonel.

*(The soldier begins running
down the mountain towards the
base camp tent. Inside the
tent, Colonel P. Chekov is
playing a game of pontoon
with a Junior Sergeant
Smithsky. The Colonel is a*

*tall man in his forties with
a gaunt face and large white
teeth.)*

JNR SGT. SMITHSKY
21 again, I don't believe your luck,
and with three sevens this time. I
don't know how you do it, I thought I
was going to win for sure with two
aces and an eight.

COLONEL P. CHEKOV
It's easy to win every time when you
cheat...

*(The Colonel takes some money
from the table and puts it in
his pocket.)*

...How about a quick game of find the
lady before you go back on duty.

JNR SGT. SMITHSKY
I better not, I promised I would take
Katerina to the cinema this weekend
when I get my pass. If I play any
more cards with you, I will have no
more money and she will have to go by
herself.

COLONEL P. CHEKOV
I would not like to see that happen.
It is bad enough you are away from
her so often. Young women are easily

lead astray by a stranger with money. It must be tough to be away from her so much, especially when there are so many of your fellow countrymen back home with idle hands and deep pockets. If you are not careful she will marry another man while you are away on tour fighting for your country.

                JNR. SGT. SMITHSKY
What are you saying?

                COLONEL P. CHEKOV
Women are fickle, and more importantly they love to nest...

        (The Colonel reaches for a
        cigar from a box covered with
        postage stamps from Cuba. He
        lights it and smiles.)

...If you are not careful, when you return home you will find she is 6 months pregnant with another man's child...

        (The Colonel puffs thick
        balls of smoke in the air and
        grins widely then laughs.)

...She will even convince you that you are the father, even when she has given the baby the surname of your best friend.

*(Jnr. Sgt Smithsky looks
quite concerned by the
Colonel's words and nervously
fumbles with the last of his
change.)*

JNR. SGT. SMITHSKY
Katerina is not like that. She would
never do such a thing...

*(Jnr. Sgt. Smithsky reaches
inside his overcoat and
passes the Colonel a letter.)*

...Look, she wrote me this letter.

*(The Colonel starts to read
the letter.)*

COLONEL P. CHEKOV
Dear Marat, I miss you so much...

*(The Colonel stops reading
and looks at the Jnr. Sgt.
Smithsky.)*

...I thought your first name was
Sergei?

JNR. SGT. SMITHSKY
It is. She has even referred to me
as Peter and Spartak in the past with
previous letters. I don't know why
she has so much trouble with my name

but the letters are always a reminder
of how much she misses me and can't
wait for my return. The wrong name
at the top of the letter is
incidental...

> *(Jnr. Sgt. Smithsky smiles
> and takes back the letter.)*

...In one letter, she even got the
address wrong and spoke of a romantic
weekend at a boathouse. She is so
funny and absent minded, we have
never been to a boathouse. In fact,
whenever I get a pass I never have
any money to go anywhere nice and we
always end up at the local café with
lemon tea and fake cream buns...

> *(Jnr. Sgt. Smithsky folds up
> the letter and places it back
> in his pocket.)*

...But this time when I get my pass
we will go to the cinema and watch a
John Wayne western.

COLONEL P. CHEKOV
A western? I bet she can't wait for
that.

> *(The tent flap opens and a
> soldier walks in.)*

                    SOLDIER 2
Colonel? We have found something in
the snow, a strange body.

        *(The Colonel looks up at the
        soldier.)*

                COLONEL P. CHEKOV
A body you say?

                    SOLDIER 2
Yes sir, but it's not human.

                COLONEL P. CHEKOV
Not human, you must have found my
mother-in-law. I believe she fits
into that category...

        *(The Colonel gets up from his
        chair, lays his cigar in an
        ashtray, puts on his overcoat
        and takes a drink of Budgie
        vodka from a bottle on the
        table.)*

...C'mon, show me where this body is.
Smithsky, you stay here. I am
waiting to hear from General
Spuriovsky and I do not want to miss
his call.

                JNR. SGT. SMITHSKY
Yes, sir.

*(The Colonel follows the
soldier up the mountainside.
After ten minutes of walking
over soft snow and craggy
rocks they reach a body lying
in the snow. The sun beams
across the landscape and the
snowy scene comes to life.)*

                    SOLDIER 1
Sir, he is still breathing. He has
been saying something but I can't
understand it.

                    COLONEL P. CHEKOV
So, you have established it is a he?

                    SOLDIER 1
I just presumed.

                    COLONEL P. CHEKOV
Presume nothing. Now, move out of
the way and let me have a look at
this thing...

*(The soldier moves to one
side and the Colonel goes
down on one knee to look at
the body. The alien is 5ft
2" tall and has large oval
eyes with a rough grey skin.
It is wearing a silver
coloured space suit and a
helmet that has a broken*

visor.)

...Odd looking fellow. Reminds me of
my cousin Feodore, he had big eyes
and a small stature. If I remember
correctly, he had a strange obsession
with collecting cruet sets...

*(The Colonel uses a nasal
spray and looks over the
body.)*

...let's see if he has any papers on
him.

*(The Colonel starts to search
the body and the alien
speaks.)*

                    ALIEN
Em-Pleh!

                    SOLDIER 2
He is trying to say something.

*(The Colonel looks at both of
the soldiers.)*

                COLONEL P. CHEKOV
You two? Go back to base camp and
fetch a stretcher. We will move him
into my tent.

SOLDIER 1 AND 2
Yes, sir.

*(The soldiers run off down
the mountain and the Colonel
searches the alien's body.)*

ALIEN
De-pÁc-se ev-ah I, Eerf mÁ I.

COLONEL P. CHEKOV
Sorry, can't understand a word, your
voice is like a tape player on fast
forward. Eh, what's this?

*(The Colonel removes a gold
key that's attached to a
chain from the alien's
pocket. He continues to
rifle the body and removes
what looks like a gold watch
from the alien's wrist.)*

ALIEN
LAS, Emod EHt...

*(The alien takes its last
breath and dies. The Colonel
continues to extract stuff
out of the alien's pockets
and also removes a ring from
the aliens left hand.)*

                    SOLDIER 1
We are here!

        (*Soldiers 1 and 2 have
        returned and they are out of
        breath.*)

                COLONEL P. CHEKOV
You are too late. He is dead. Take
the alien back to the base camp and
throw him in a body bag.

        (*The Colonel gets to his feet
        and starts to walk down the
        mountain.*)

                    SOLDIER 1
Oh, Colonel? Jnr. Sgt. Smithsky told
me to tell you that General
Spuriovsky is on his way.

                COLONEL P. CHEKOV
Oh, yes, the General. I almost
forgot about him. Tell the other men
to keep looking on the mountain,
there might be another body and there
must be a ship around here somewhere.

                    SOLDIER 1
Yes, sir.

Scene fades.

ACT 1, SCENE 3

2.05pm. Saturday 18th October 2025, The Red Square, Moscow. General Spuriovsky's men are busy ransacking the shops and looking under every counter top to find Dmitry, Yuri and the aliens. The Moon Man is awoken by the noise and stands up to look outside. MacTavish begins to sing again with great fervour and passion and gets to his feet.

MOON MAN
Whatever is that racket?

MACTAVISH
There was a young wifie fae weegie toon, who laughed sae hard her bloomers fell doon...

(MacTavish takes a swig of leather cleaner and continues to sing.)

...When she tried tae collect them, what a sight we all saw, when she tumbled ower and fell tae the floor.

(General Spuriovsky's men are alerted by MacTavish's singing and enter the clothes shop.)

SOLDIER A
Nobody move and put your hands up.

MOON MAN
How can we put our hands up if we
can't move?

SOLDIER B
Silence...

> (Soldier B runs out onto the
> street.)

...General, we have found the aliens.

GENERAL SPURIOVSKY
Good. Keep them there, I am
coming...

> (The General enters the shop.
> MacTavish is still singing.)

...What is wrong with this one?

SOLDIER A
He seems to be drunk on leather
cleaner, sir.

GENERAL SPURIOVSKY
Leather cleaner? I have never tried
it myself, so I cannot judge...

> (The General looks at the
> Moon Man. His wig covers his

face and his hat is drooping
to one side.)

...What's the story with this other
one?

                SOLDIER A
Don't know, sir, but he speaks
Russian.

           GENERAL SPURIOVSKY
That is good to hear...

     (The General looks at the
     Moon Man.)

...Where are you from?

               MOON MAN
Vlogomvich.

           GENERAL SPURIOVSKY
Is that close to planet Earth?

               MOON MAN
What do you mean close to Earth?
It's on it. It's about 65 miles away
as the crow flies...

     (The Moon Man straightens his
     wig and puts his hat on.)

...'ere what's your game, you don't
think I'm one of them do you?

(*General Spuriovsky looks at
the Moon Man and starts to
smile.*)

GENERAL SPURIOVSKY
My apologies, I can see you are a
woman. Private Kuznetsov informed me
he had found the aliens we were
looking for. With your hair in front
of your face, I didn't know what to
expect...

(*The General plays with his
moustache and lifts his
shoulders.*)

...Now I can see your face, it is
clear you are an Earthling, and may I
be as bold to say a very attractive
one at that.

MOON MAN
Ooh, you may...

(*The Moon Man applies some
lipstick and smiles at the
General.*)

...And may I say that is a very smart
uniform you are wearing, and such
nice badges, reminds me a bit of the
Boy Scouts. Are you an admiral or
something?

(The General is a little
cross for a moment then
smiles.)

GENERAL SPURIOVSKY
An admiral, no. An admiral is in
charge of a fleet in the navy. I am
a general.

MOON MAN
A general? You must be ever so
important?

(MacTavish starts to sing
again.)

A little...

(The General looks at
MacTavish then back at the
Moon Man.)

...But tell me, what are you doing
here with this alien?

MOON MAN
Nothing! There I was, minding me own
business shopping for a new frock,
and then...

(The Moon Man puts his arms
in the air.)

...Big explosions, glass shattering

and total chaos all around. This
one...

> *(The Moon Man points at
> MacTavish.)*

...Comes running in here with that
white fellow and all that English
Riff-Raff pushing and shoving like a
load of old furniture removal men.
All I wanted was to go to the Autumn
Festival and buy a new frock, now
look at me?

GENERAL SPURIOVSKY
Why, you are trembling. This all
must be very unsettling for you...

> *(The Moon Man takes a
> handkerchief and wipes his
> eyes.)*

...There, there sweet child...

> *(The General takes the Moon
> Man by the hand.)*

...You are safe now. Is there
anywhere I can take you? Do you need
a ride home?

> *(MacTavish starts to sing
> again and moves his arms out
> towards the General. The
> General looks at the*

Private.)

...Private? Take this fool away and
put him in the back of the truck.

                    SOLDIER A
Yes, sir.

        *(The Private escorts
        MacTavish into the back of
        one of the trucks - MacTavish
        continues to sing.)*

                    MOON MAN
What about this one?

                    GENERAL SPURIOVSKY
What one?

                    MOON MAN
The white funny looking one on the
floor down here at me feet, as hard
as a rock.

        *(The General moves some
        handbags and clothes rails
        out of the way and walks to
        where the Moon Man is
        standing. He shouts out to
        the Private.)*

                    GENERAL SPURIOVSKY
Private?

SOLDIER A
Come and get this other fellow, there
is another one...

> *(The General stares at the*
> *Moon Man's legs.)*

...Why, what attractive long legs you
have.

> *(The General stands up*
> *straight. A couple of*
> *soldiers enter the shop and*
> *take KAL's body out and put*
> *it into the back of the*
> *truck.)*

MOON MAN
Why thank you. You are the first one
to notice.

GENERAL SPURIOVSKY
Surely not... Now, I was saying.
Can we drop you somewhere?

MOON MAN
Well, I was going to catch the bus
back home, but my purse was stolen by
those English reprobates, so I don't
know what I am going to do now.

GENERAL SPURIOVSKY
Who are these English fellows you are
speaking of?

                    MOON MAN
A load of brutes and thugs from the
gutter I should think, out on the
town to cause trouble. They just
came running in here like a load of
sheep fleeing a wolf. They knocked
me out and stole my purse. I woke up
when you arrived. I've probably
missed the bus home now.

                GENERAL SPURIOVSKY
I am afraid the bus service has been
cancelled due to the alien invasion.

                    MOON MAN
What? Do you mean there are more of
them?

                GENERAL SPURIOVSKY
Quite possibly, but we are still
looking. The roads out of Moscow
have also been closed and we are
going to put the city under martial
law until further notice, so I am
afraid you won't be able to go home
for a couple of days.

                    MOON MAN
Oh, my poor old mother is there by
herself.

        (The Moon Man looks anxious.)

GENERAL SPURIOVSKY
Perhaps I can help...

(The General puts his hand to his mouth and coughs.)

...I have a castle a few miles outside of Moscow. It is a modest place, but it has the basics. The electricity is out in the city due to our current crisis, so I will be staying there for a couple of days. You are welcome to join me. I am sure I can get a local policeman to look in on your mother and bring her supplies.

MOON MAN
Well, that does sound very generous, but I have nothing to wear?

GENERAL SPURIOVSKY
Do not worry about that. We can get you some new clothes sent out to the castle. It's the least I can do.

MOON MAN
Well, how can I refuse. I accept your most generous offer.

GENERAL SPURIOVSKY
Good, then that is settled...

(The General takes the Moon

*Man's arm and they walk out
of the shop and get into the
back of his jeep. A Sergeant
from the platoon approaches
the General.)*

...Keep looking for the two
cosmonauts Sergeant and keep me
appraised of your progress. I want
this area searched thoroughly by
night fall. Have the aliens
delivered to my castle and contact
Anisimov and have him meet us there.

                    SERGEANT
Very good, sir.

          *(The Sergeant starts to walk
          away.)*

                    GENERAL SPURIOVSKY
Oh, and Sergeant?...

          *(The Sergeant walks back to
          the General.)*

...Keep an eye open for a group of
English men roaming around. They
have stolen this lady's purse, and I
want it found.

                    SERGEANT
Very good, sir. I'll inform the
platoon.

(The Sergeant walks away.)

        GENERAL SPURIOVSKY
When you are ready Corporal?

*(A Corporal, who sits in the
driver's seat, starts the
jeep and they drive off. The
Moon Man snuggles up to the
General as they drive down
the street.)*

Scene fades.

ACT 1, SCENE 4

2.24pm. Saturday 18th October 2025, Nikoslava Street, Moscow. London and his group of ex-SAS soldiers have been dodging in and out of the shadows for the past 20 minutes avoiding military patrols and newly formed groups of militia. Up ahead, they notice a pawnbrokers shop with a collapsed frontage and an open door. They decide to make this their destination. They are about to move out of the shadows of a small alley when a loud siren is heard followed by the sound of several tanks and armoured vehicles moving towards their vicinity. From a P.A. system mounted on a tank, an announcement echoes throughout the streets.

P.A. SYSTEM
Acting under emergency orders issued by President Putovsky to initiate and implement the alien invasion act of 1964, code B-486/F, the city of Moscow has now been placed under martial law. Military forces under the command of General Spuriovsky will be stationed throughout the city to enforce law and order and keep the peace. As of 7pm this evening, a curfew will be initiated and remain operative until further notice. Anyone caught on the streets after

this time without the necessary
permit to travel will be arrested.
Any civilians caught looting from
shops or homes will be shot on sight.
All utility services such as gas,
electric and telephone have been
suspended for your safety and will be
restored when the necessary repair
work has been completed. Thank you
for your cooperation.

> (The P.A. System makes a loud
> screeching sound and is
> replaced by the thunder of
> military vehicles and
> marching troops moving in the
> direction of London and his
> men.)

                    LONDON
I don't think we can hang around here
much longer. We better get going.

                  CARTWRIGHT
I don't think I can go on much
further. I don't mind missing the
odd meal, but at my age, well, I like
regular meal times.

                    LONDON
Yes, well, these things can't be
helped. You should have taken some
of that German chaps food when we
were in the balloon. Winslow managed

to stuff a whole ham down his throat
and a loaf of pumpernickel. You
should of grabbed some of that when
you had the chance.

                    CARTWRIGHT
Well maybe I would have if I'd
thought he was going to eat the lot.

                    LONDON
I can't imagine why you are bringing
this up now when we are in this jam.
You should be taking this up with
Winslow not me, I'm just as hungry as
you are...

        *(London turns and faces
        Cartwright.)*

...Look Cartwright, we all know
things haven't gone quite to plan...

        (Cavendish interjects.)

                    CAVENDISH
Do you think?

                    LONDON
Don't you start Cavendish, I'm in the
mood for a right good punch up.

                    CAVENDISH
Anytime, London.

LONDON
Look out, someone's coming!

(*Two Russian soldiers walk
towards where they are
crouched down in an alleyway.
The soldiers stop to light a
cigarette and notice
something moving in the
shadows. London leaps to his
feet, punches one of the
soldiers in the face, grabs
his rifle and hits the other
one with its butt. Both
soldiers fall to the floor
unconscious.*)

LONDON
Well don't just sit there, give me a
hand with the bodies!...

(*Cavendish and the rest are
struck dumb by London's quick
action to take out the
Russian soldiers and have a
look of wonderment and
surprise on their faces.*)

...Well, c'mon, don't just sit there
gaping like monkeys. Give me a hand
before anyone else comes along.

(*Cavendish, Carter and
Cartwright help London pick
up the bodies. They carry*

*them off of the street and
into a florist shop.)*

CAVENDISH
Nice work London. You've just bagged
us a couple of AK-47's.

LONDON
Better check them over for other
stuff. See if they've got any money
or travel documents.

*(Cavendish and Carter check
over the bodies. Carter
finds some boiled sweets,
spare ammo and a wrist watch.
Cavendish finds some military
papers, a train timetable and
some cash.)*

CARTER
That's more like it, 10,000 rubles.

LONDON
What else have you found?

CARTER
Some spare ammo, a wrist watch and
some boiled sweets.

LONDON
Good. And what about you Cavendish,
what treasures have you found?

CAVENDISH
A train timetable, military papers
and some cash, about 5,000 Rubles.

LONDON
Excellent. You better share out the
boiled sweets before Cartwright goes
to sleep...

    (Cavendish hands out an equal
    amount of boiled sweets to
    everyone - three each.)

...Rhubarb and Custard. Just the
ticket to raise the spirits, what?

CARTWRIGHT
I don't suppose there are any other
flavours, like beef stew. I've never
really liked rhubarb.

LONDON
I guess there's no pleasing some
people. Let's have a look at those
military papers Cavendish.

CAVENDISH
Can you read Russian?

LONDON
Enough to grasp the situation, why?

                    CAVENDISH
I just wondered if you'd watched any
Russian war movies, that was all.

                     LONDON
I've seen the odd one, but my
mother's father could speak and read
Russian quite well and he taught me a
line or two. So, if you have quite
finished checking my qualifications,
could I see the papers...

          *(Cavendish hands over the
          military papers. London
          looks them over.)*

...This is a stroke of luck. These
are travel documents issued by some
chap called General Spuriovsky. They
give the holder permission to travel
throughout the city. This could come
in handy if we get caught in a spot
of bother.

                   PILKINGTON
Won't they be a bit suspicious of six
Englishmen dressed in civilian
clothing wandering around in the city
with a Russian military travel pass.

                     LONDON
Yes, I suppose they might do...

          (London looks over to

*Pilkington and then at one of
the Russian soldiers.)*

...How tall are you Pilky?

PILKINGTON
Five foot seven and a half.

LONDON
Good. I would say you are the same
size as this chap on the floor here,
and Winslow looks to be about the
size of the other. Right you two, we
have no time to lose, off with
everything. C'mon, swap clothes with
these two Russian fellows as soon as
you can.

WINSLOW
What?

LONDON
You heard me Winslow. We just can't
wander around the streets anymore
waiting to be caught, we have to take
charge of the situation instead of
scurrying about the gutters like a
load of hungry rats. Two Russian
soldiers escorting some civilians out
of the area wouldn't look out of
place at all...

*(London pops a rhubarb and
custard sweet into his mouth*

and takes a look at the train
timetable.)

...In fact, it's the perfect cover.
As long as nobody stops us we'll be
fine.

CARTER
It sounds good to me, but what about
these two?...

(Carter points at the two
Russian soldiers on the
floor.)

...Shall I slit their throats?

LONDON
There'll be no slitting of throats
Carter, not unless it's absolutely
necessary.

CAVENDISH
Could be a mistake keeping them
alive, might even be our downfall.

LONDON
I appreciate what you are saying
Cavendish, but please remember who we
are. We are not a gang of mindless
hooligans out on a rampage, we're
British. I'm not about to give an
order to kill two unconscious men.
Just take off their clothes, tie them

up, give them another cosh on the head and throw them into a store cupboard. That should hold them for a few hours. We shall be long gone before they wake up to alert anyone.

                    CARTER
Long gone? Where are we going to go exactly?

                    LONDON
Well Carter, you do surprise me. I would have thought it was obvious?

                    CAVENDISH
Well perhaps you could enlighten the rest of us plebs as well.

                    LONDON
The train station.

                    CARTER
The train station?...

        (Carter starts to walk about
        the shop.)

...What did I tell you. I knew we'd have to find our own way home and pay for it ourselves.

                    LONDON
Look Carter, you heard the

announcement the same as I did.
There is no power and no phones. The
railway station on the other hand has
emergency generators and a radio
transmitter in the Station Master's
office. According to this map, we
are only 20 minutes from the
Lengrasky Station. If we are lucky,
we just might be able to get into
that office and contact H.Q. to
arrange another pickup.

*(Winslow and Pilkington have
finished swapping clothes
with the Russian soldiers and
have moved the bodies into a
back storage room.)*

CARTER
It all sounds a bit risky to me.
This place is going to be swarming
with troops before too long.

LONDON
Well, we can't stay here, there's no
cover and no back door. I suggest we
push on to the top of this road and
get into that pawnbrokers shop and
wait until it gets dark.

CARTER
What's so special about that place?

LONDON
Well, I'll tell you shall I Carter.
There is bound to be a back door and
a basement to hide in to start with.
We would be extremely unlucky not to
find any weapons. I imagine that
sort of establishment is always
selling and buying guns and knives,
might even find the odd grenade.

CAVENDISH
He's right Carter, there could be all
sorts of stuff, *walkie-talkies*, spare
ammo, body armour and the best thing
- there's bound to be clothes we can
change into. I don't know about you
lot, but I wouldn't mind a change of
clothes and a warm coat!

LONDON
Right then, that's settled. Let's
get going!

*(London and his team of ex-
SAS soldiers walk out onto
the street. Winslow and
Pilkington walk behind them
with the rifles over their
shoulders.)*

CARTWRIGHT
I can hear something, footsteps.

(London and his men carry on

walking up the street when
they are met with a platoon
of Russian soldiers.)

WINSLOW
Prodolzhayte dvigat'sya, inache vas
zastrelyat!

(Winslow nods at the passing
platoon and pushes Cavendish
in the back with his rifle.
They walk a bit further and
stop outside the pawnbrokers
shop.)

LONDON
I say Winslow, I didn't know you
could speak Russian?

WINSLOW
I can't, I just remembered a line
from an old war movie I'd seen.

CAVENDISH
Where would we be without the movies.
What did you say?

WINSLOW
I told you to keep moving or you
would be shot!

LONDON
Good show Winslow. You've certainly

saved the day.

> (Down the street a commotion
> has started. Two men wearing
> only their underwear and
> bound in ropes have fallen
> into the street. They are
> shouting out for help. The
> nearby Russian platoon comes
> to their assistance. London
> looks down the street at the
> scene.)

LONDON
Quick inside, we've been rumbled...

> (London and his men enter the
> shop and board up the
> entrance with rubble and
> debris.)

...That should get them off our scent
for a while.

> (Outside in the street a
> vehicle stops suddenly,
> voices are heard shouting and
> the sound of dogs barking
> fill the alleyways.)

Scene fades.

ACT 1, SCENE 5

2.26pm.   Saturday 18th October 2025,
Trovsky Street, Moscow.   Dmitry and
Yuri have taken cover under a coffee
shop awning for a moment.   Around
them, soldiers continue to burst into
shops and search for undesirables and
looters.   Over in another street, they
hear the end announcement from a P.A.
system.

                    YURI
Did you hear that Dmitry, there is
going to be a curfew.

                    DMITRY
Yes, and it sounds like they will
shoot first and ask questions later.
We better find somewhere to hold up.
There is only a few hours of daylight
left and it looks like a storm is
brewing.

          (Marching is heard up the
          street from their position
          and Dmitry and Yuri duck down
          behind a shop sign promoting
          cappuccinos made from
          dandelion root.)

                    YURI
Where would you like to go Dmitry?
What about the Ritz-Carlton hotel? I

believe they have good room service and an excellent dessert menu.

(Dmitry begins to smile.)

                    DMITRY
I think it was damaged by that alien spaceship, what about the Marriot Grand hotel, that is still standing? They have an amazing fish restaurant with a free bar.

                    YURI
Sounds good. The Marriot it is.

                    DMITRY
Sorry Yuri, I have just remembered we won't be able to get in without a tie.

                    YURI
Then I guess we better spend the night sleeping in steel dumpster foraging for food in garbage bags.

(They both laugh.)

                    DMITRY
I don't know why we are making jokes, our situation is pretty dire.

(The sound of a voice shouting is heard. Mrs. Plumitry and her small group

of militia arrive on the
street.)

MRS PLUMITRY
It's probably best we split up into
groups of four...

(Mrs Plumitry points at three
people.)

...You three come with me and the
rest can go with Mr Applebag.

MR. APPLEBAG
I think it's best if we all stick
together. I don't want to be
mistaken as a looter.

MRS. PLUMITRY
Mr. Applebag, I don't think anyone
could mistake you for a looter, you
are 87 years old, walk with a cane
and have a pacemaker. You are just
being silly. Now, be off with you.

(Mr. Applebag and his group
move away from the area and
walk down a side street.
Mrs. Plumitry and her group
continue to walk on the main
thoroughfare towards Dmitry
and Yuri.)

                    DMITRY
Yuri, they are coming towards us,
let's get going.

        *(Yuri stands up and knocks
        over some chairs and a table
        that were stacked next to
        them. They crash to the
        ground with a loud clatter
        and roll out into the
        street.)*

                    YURI
Run for it Dmitry!

        *(Mrs. Plumitry sees Yuri and
        Dmitry and they quickly get
        to their feet.)*

                MRS. PLUMITRY
There they are. After them!

        *(Mrs. Plumitry and her group
        of three run towards Yuri and
        Dmitry at full speed. After
        10 seconds, they begin
        walking briskly and begin
        breathing heavily and stop
        for a short rest.)*

                GROUP MEMBER 1
They're getting a way!

MRS. PLUMITRY
Let's wait here a minute, maybe
they'll circle back in our direction
and we can catch them as they run by.

GROUP MEMBER 2
Do you think that is likely?

MRS. PLUMITRY
Goblins are just like rabid dogs,
they always run around in circles.

GROUP MEMBER 1
Do you really think they are goblins,
they looked pretty real to me.

MRS. PLUMITRY
That's the trick with goblins, they
are clever and cunning - shape
shifters some of them.

(Dmitry and Yuri run down a
narrow alleyway straight into
an open street. They see Mr.
Applebag and the other group
and move out of sight. On
the other side of the street,
a platoon of soldiers are
gathering up some looters. A
Sergeant Ciderovsky calls out
to Mr. Applebag.)

SERGEANT CIDEROVSKY
You there! What are you doing in

this area?

                    MR. APPLEBAG
Who me?

          SERGEANT CIDEROVSKY
Yes you. Don't you know this area is
restricted?

                    MR. APPLEBAG
Yes, but we are part of the militia
looking for the two doppelgangers.

          SERGEANT CIDEROVSKY
The doppel- what?

                    MR. APPLEBAG
The two aliens that have taken on
human form.

          (Dmitry and Yuri's attention
          is taken away from Mr.
          Applebag and the Sergeant
          when some soldiers begin
          lining up eight civilian men
          against a wall. At their
          feet, television sets, oil
          paintings, silverware,
          musical instruments and
          kitchen stools lay
          scattered.)

                    SERGEANT CIDEROVSKY
Don't know anything about that...

            (The Sergeant calls over a
            Private Blake.)

...Do you know anything about aliens
that have taken on human form?

                    PRIVATE BLAKE
No, *Sarg*. Sounds like a bit of a
tall tale to me. They must be
looters. You can tell just by
looking at them. Especially this old
scrawny one with the cane. Typical
jewel thief if ever there was.

                    MR. APPLEBAG
What, I'm not a jewel thief. I'm
part of the militia.

                    PRIVATE BLAKE
It's nonsense *Sarg.*, put them
against the wall with the other lot.

                    SERGEANT CIDEROVSKY
Right, you heard what he said.
Against the wall with the others.

            (Mr. Applebag and his gang
            walk over to the wall and
            join the eight men.)

                    YURI
Dmitry, they are going to shoot them!

                   DMITRY
Better them than us.

                    YURI
But they are not looters?

                   DMITRY
No, they are worse. They are deluded
homicidal maniacs on the hunt for
goblins. What do you think would've
happened if they'd caught us. Do you
think they would believe story of
fabulous space adventure and set us
free?

                    YURI
No, I don't suppose they would have
done that.

                   DMITRY
Sometimes Yuri, you are too soft.
Look at the fix we are in. We have
no one to turn to, no food or bed for
the night and we could be killed at
any moment, and you are bothered
about some old man and his gang.
Wise up Yuri!

                    YURI
I am not like you Dmitry, it is true,

but I am not soft...

> (*Rifle fire rings out through the streets and the twelve men fall to the ground dead. Yuri grabs Dmitry.*)

...Dmitry!

> ### DMITRY

Watch what you are doing, you have pinched my skin! Let's get out of here before we end up them like those goblin hunters.

> (*An army jeep pulls up next to Sergeant Ciderovsky and a Corporal Pip gets out. They salute one another and the Corporal hands over a piece of paper.*)

> ### CORPORAL PIP

New orders, sir from General Spuriovsky.

> (*The Sergeant reads the new orders.*)

> ### DMITRY

Wait a minute Yuri, let's listen to the orders. We might learn something about their manoeuvres.

*(The Sergeant addresses his
platoon.)*

SERGEANT CIDEROVSKY
Attention! We have just received
word from General Spuriovsky to be on
the lookout for two fugitives known
as Yuri Chekov and Dmitry Usakov. It
is believed they are armed and
dangerous and possibly of alien
origin. It is recommended we
approach them with extreme caution.
There is also a further report from
General Spuriovsky regarding a stolen
handbag. Earlier today, a group of
men, believed to be English, stole a
handbag from a civilian shopper.
These men are wanted for questioning
regarding this matter and are to be
arrested on sight...

*(The Sergeant folds the piece
of paper.)*

...So, keep your eyes peeled, and be
on the lookout for any suspicious
characters.

*(Private Blake addresses
Sergeant Ciderovsky.)*

PRIVATE BLAKE
You don't suppose that chap we just

shot was telling the truth do you?

                    SERGEANT CIDEROVSKY
Too late now...

        (The Sergeant looks at his
        men.)

...Right, let's move out.

        (Grey clouds begin to move
        over the city and it begins
        to rain. Yuri and Dmitry run
        into a courtyard and see the
        back entrance to a public
        house. The door is open and
        a few abandoned barrels lay
        scattered about.)

                    DMITRY
Look! It is a pub...

        (Dmitry reads a sign above
        the door.)

    ...'The Dragon's Breath' - That is a
good name for a pub, much better than
most. In my father's town of
Levkoko, they have a pub called, 'The
Bear and the Saucepan'. What a
stupid name; and the beer was served
warm. This place doesn't look bad
from out here.

                    YURI
I don't think we should be drinking
just now Dmitry.

        *(Storm clouds start to gather
        and the light dims. Moments
        later, hailstones begin
        bouncing off the ground like
        tiny ping pong balls and a
        crack of thunder is heard.
        Flashes of spider lightning
        fill the sky and a single
        ground strike hits a nearby
        building. A blue neon street
        sign momentarily bursts into
        life with the words - 'THE
        PARROT CLUB', then tumbles
        down to the ground and
        crashes through a shop
        window.)*

                    DMITRY
Quickly, let's get inside.

        *(Dmitry and Yuri run inside
        the pub and close the door
        behind them.)*

                    YURI
That is better. Under the present
circumstances, it looks like a good
place to hold up for a few hours...

        *(Yuri begins to look around
        and notices a cigarette*

vending machine.)

...I could use a smoke.

DMITRY
And I could use a drink...

*(In front of Dmitry is a long
bar filled with alcohol.)*

...It looks like there is going to be
a free bar after all.

YURI
That is good, but I would have
enjoyed a good fish meal to
complement the wine. What a shame we
couldn't find a tie.

(They both laugh.)

Scene fades.

ACT 1, SCENE 6

3.08pm. Saturday 18th October, 2025. A covered military truck and a jeep transporting General Spuriovsky and the Moon Man drive through the village of Alabino, 30 miles south-west of Moscow. The sun is shining, but the air temperature is cold and pockets of iced puddles can be seen on the pavements. Out of town, The vehicles turn up an estate road leading to General Spuriovsky's castle on the top of Sparrow Hill.

GENERAL SPURIOVSKY
You are cold my dear. Here take this blanket.

(The General hands the Moon
Man a woollen blanket.)

MOON MAN
Thank you. I've all of a sudden got cold.

GENERAL SPURIOVSKY
I should have realised. We have climbed a good 500 feet since Moscow. The air temperature up here is much colder and takes a bit of getting used to but we are nearly at my castle. You will soon get warm in front of the fire.

(The vehicles pull up in front of a huge building with an octagonal shape and eight large turrets. In the centre, a glass cupola adorns the structure and two sets of steps lead up to the main entrance.)

MOON MAN
Oh, ain't it lovely.

GENERAL SPURIOVSKY
Yes, it has been in my family for over 400 years...

(The General exits the jeep and helps the Moon Man out and begins to address the Corporal.)

...Will you see that...

(The General looks back to the Moon Man.)

...Forgive me, but we have been engaged in conversation for the last 40 minutes and I have not even enquired after your name.

MOON MAN
My name?

                    GENERAL SPURIOVSKY
Yes, your name.

                        MOON MAN
It is... It is Sam.

                    GENERAL SPURIOVSKY
Sam?

        (The Moon Man looks nervous
        and agitated.)

                        MOON MAN
Yes, it is short for Samantha.

        (The General smiles and
        kisses the Moon Man's left
        hand.)

                    GENERAL SPURIOVSKY
Oh, I see. That is a nice name, but
I think I will call you my little
Pomidor.

                        MOON MAN
Oh, Pomidor, I like that. I have
always been partial to a bit of
fruit.

        (The General releases the
        Moon Man's hand and turns to
        face the Corporal.)

GENERAL SPURIOVSKY
As I was saying, will you escort our
guest to the main living quarters and
see she is taken care of.

CORPORAL
Very good General, I will see to it
right away.

*(General Spuriovsky turns
back to face the Moon Man.)*

GENERAL SPURIOVSKY
Please forgive me for a short while.
I have some very important business
to attend to. I will join you
shortly.

MOON MAN
Until then.

*(The Moon Man blows the
General a kiss and walks away
with the corporal. General
Spuriovsky walks to the back
of the truck. A Private
Vanisky is trying to restrain
KAL.)*

GENERAL SPURIOVSKY
What is happening Private?

*(Private Vanisky continues to
wrestle with KAL.)*

PRIVATE VANISKY
This white chap has come back to life
and is trying to break free. He has
snapped his handcuffs and knocked out
Private Trout.

*(General Spuriovsky takes out
his sidearm and fires next to
KAL's head. KAL stops
fighting.)*

GENERAL SPURIOVSKY
Move away from him Private.

*(Private Vanisky moves back
and sits on a bench seat
inside the truck. The
General holds his pistol
firmly at KAL and addresses
him.)*

GENERAL SPURIOVSKY
Do you understand what I am saying,
can you speak Russian.

KAL
I speak most languages from this
planet.

GENERAL SPURIOVSKY
Good. Then this should be easy. You
and your sleeping friend here...

(The General pokes MacTavish

with his pistol.)

...are my prisoners. You have been
brought here for questioning. Do as
I say and no harm will come to you.
If you try to escape, you will be
killed. Do you understand?

                    KAL
Yes.

                GENERAL SPURIOVSKY
Good. Carry on private...

(Private Trout wakes up.)

...Glad you could join us. Now, take
these two to the dungeon and throw
them in a cell. I want a guard
posted outside at all times. Make
sure they get some food and fresh
clothes.

                PRIVATE VANISKY
Yes, General.

        *(Private Trout and Vanisky
        walk KAL and MacTavish to the
        back of the castle and
        disappear out of sight.
        General Spuriovsky lights a
        cigarette and begins to walk
        back to the castle when he
        sees a car coming up the*

hill. He waits on the
driveway for the car to
arrive. To pass the time, he
dances and begins to sing to
himself.)

GENERAL SPURIOVSKY

There was a drunk sailor who slipped on the deck,
he shouted out loudly, 'I've hurt my poor neck'.

Then a wave crashed over and swept him away,
and the crew they all sang, 'There'll be rum left today.'

Fa-la-la diddly um dum fa-la-la diddly ay,
there's many a drunk in the Locker they say.

So you better be cautious, you better take care,
if you don't watch your step, you'll soon be down there.

Fa-la-la diddle um dum fa-la-la diddly ay,
there's many a drunk in the Locker they say...

(A car pulls into the
driveway, A black Zil-117. A
chauffer gets out and opens
the back door. A tall thin
man in his late 50's exits.
He is dressed in a black suit
and tie and has a thin Prince
moustache. He takes a
cigarette from a silver
holder and lights it. The
General puts out his
cigarette and walks over to

him and they shake hands.)

GENERAL SPURIOVSKY
Anisimov, it is good to see you. I
am glad you could come at such short
notice.

ANISIMOV
You called, so I came.

GENERAL SPURIOVSKY
You look well, the textile and floor
covering business must be good for
you.

ANISIMOV
It is, and the work is much cleaner.

*(They walk towards the
castle.)*

GENERAL SPURIOVSKY
How is your wife, Katriana?

ANISIMOV
She is dead.

GENERAL SPURIOVSKY
I am sorry to hear that, Anisimov.
How did your wife die?

ANISIMOV
I killed her. She was cheating on me

with one of my employees, a carpet
fitter. I shot the both of them and
threw the bodies in the Volga river.

                GENERAL SPURIOVSKY
A carpet fitter, that is too bad.

                ANISIMOV
It is, he was a good man. Do you
know how difficult it is to get
decent carpet fitters these days?

        (General Spuriovsky and
        Anisimov enter the castle
        hallway and are met by a
        butler.)

                GENERAL SPURIOVSKY
This is Godfrey, my butler. If you
need anything, just ask.

        (Godfrey looks at Anisimov.)

                GODFREY
Would you like me to get your luggage
from the car, sir?

                ANISIMOV
Yes, the driver will give you a hand.

                GODFREY
Very good, sir.

(*Anisimov and General
Spuriovsky walk towards the
living room.*)

GENERAL SPURIOVSKY
Would you like a drink?

ANISIMOV
Yes, but I would also like to know
why I am here?

GENERAL SPURIOVSKY
I guess there is no easy way to say
this, so I will just say it...

(*The General looks at
Anisimov.*)

...I need your help again regarding
the aliens.

(*Anisimov looks slightly
annoyed.*)

ANISIMOV
You promised me that I would not have
to be involved anymore. I was very
fond of LAX, and that whole affair
with the *bullet* and the Professor
left me very distraught. I couldn't
eat for days afterwards.

GENERAL SPURIOVSKY
Yes, I know, but I have a couple of

prisoners in the dungeon I think you
will want to meet.

                    ANISIMOV
Why?

                GENERAL SPURIOVSKY
They are aliens. Different to LAX,
but just as intriguing. They might
have some valuable information and I
trust your particular powers of
persuasion to extract it...

          (The General smiles at
          Anisimov.)

...Besides, you speak their tongue,
and they might warm to someone who
uses a familiar parlance.

                    ANISIMOV
Do you think?...

          (Anisimov loosens his tie.)

...When do we start?

                GENERAL SPURIOVSKY
First thing tomorrow morning. They
have just arrived and I want to give
them a chance to sweat a little.
Besides I have someone I would like
you to meet.

*(General Spuriovsky and
Anisimov walk into the living
room. The Moon Man is
sitting by the fire reading a
magazine.)*

GENERAL SPURIOVSKY
Ahh, there you are my little Pomidor.
I want you to meet a good friend of
mine.

*(The Moon Man gets from his
seat and General Spuriovsky
and Anisimov walk over to
him.)*

MOON MAN
Nice to meet you.

*(The Moon Man holds out his
hand and Anisimov kisses it.)*

ANISIMOV
My, what lovely skin you have, so
soft.

MOON MAN
I try to look after meself.

ANISIMOV
Yes, I can see. I am Anisimov, and
what is your name?

                    MOON MAN
I am Samantha, Sam for short.

                    ANISIMOV
That is a lovely name, it was also
the name of my first wife, but I used
to call her my little Ananas.

                    MOON MAN
Oh, another fruit name, how quaint.

                    ANISIMOV
Yes, she loved that name. It summed
her up completely; soft on the inside
with a prickly exterior. It is a
shame she has gone, she was so
beautiful.

                    MOON MAN
Did she leave you for another?

                    ANISIMOV
No, she drowned.

                    MOON MAN
Drowned! That is a 'orrible way to
die. Did she fall in a river?

                    ANISIMOV
No, a bookshelf fell on her while she
was in the bath. She was knocked
unconscious and slipped under the
water.

MOON MAN
How awful, I do feel for you. Still,
at least you are married again?

(The General raises his
eyebrows, coughs and then
walks over to the drinks
cabinet.)

GENERAL SPURIOVSKY
Can I get anyone a drink?

MOON MAN
Could I get a whisky on the rocks?

GENERAL SPURIOVSKY
Yes, certainly. And what about you
Anisimov?

ANISIMOV
I will have the same...

(Anisimov looks at the Moon
Man.)

...What about you, are you married?

MOON MAN
No, I've never been asked.

ANISIMOV
I find that very difficult to
believe. There must have been

someone?

(General Spuriovsky returns
with the drinks and hands
them out. He then walks over
to the fire and warms his
bottom.)

MOON MAN
No one I care to remember. They were
all such brutes.

ANISIMOV
Forgive me, I did not mean to pry. I
just meant to enquire why a beautiful
woman was here by herself?

GENERAL SPURIOVSKY
My little Pomidor is a guest for a
few days. She was mugged in the city
by some English thugs and I invited
her to join me at the castle until
she gets over the shock.

ANISIMOV
Oh, I see. I am very sorry to hear
that. Crime seems to be everywhere
these days and by the most unlikely
of people. Well if you will forgive
me, I am a bit tired...

(Anisimov looks at the
General.)

...I think I will finish this drink and retire to my quarters. If you can get your butler to show me the way, I will bid you farewell...

(Anisimov looks at the Moon Man.)

...Until tomorrow, madam.

MOON MAN
Yes, well, nice to meet you.

(The butler arrives and Anisimov leaves with him.)

GENERAL SPURIOVSKY
Now, my little Pomidor, can I get you another drink, a cocktail perhaps?

MOON MAN
A cocktail, well alright. I'll have a *Hanky-Panky, if you've got.*

GENERAL SPURIOVSKY
I haven't had one of those in years. Remind me what's in it again?

MOON MAN
Dry Gin, Italian Vermouth and a good dash of Fernet-Branca.

                    GENERAL SPURIOVSKY
I can see you are a girl who likes a
good time. I will join you.

                      MOON MAN
I'm always up for a good time.

        (The General fixes the Hanky-
        Panky cocktail and hands one
        to the Moon Man. He raises
        his glass and they both
        smile.)

                    GENERAL SPURIOVSKY
To my little Pomidor.

        (The glasses ting together
        and they take a drink.)

                      MOON MAN
Mmm, Lovely. Let's have another.

Scene fades.

ACT 1, SCENE 7

3.22pm. Saturday 18th October 2025, Nikoslava Street, Moscow. Rain pounds down hard against the ground and the roads begin to fill with water. The drains start to overflow and make burbling, slurping sounds as gallons of dirty liquid try to penetrate an invisible oily barrier. Inside a pawnbrokers shop, London and his group of ex-SAS soldiers search frantically amongst the merchandise for items of use. They pull out drawers filled with watches and rings, scour clothes rails and open cash boxes. They grab rifles and pistols from gun cases, smash open knife displays and take binoculars and torches from glass carousels. After a fruitful rampage, they enter the back of the shop, where they find a large refrigerator stuffed to capacity with food and beer. They sit around a kidney shaped table and go through their spoils. Carter hands out some bottles of beer and beef sandwiches and places a leg of honey smoked ham on the side. London takes out his train timetable, unfolds it and turns it over to show a map of the city. He places it on the table and everyone looks on with great enthusiasm and interest.

                    LONDON
Well, I think we can all agree that
coming to this shop was a good idea.
Not only have we managed to get some
nice warm overcoats, but we have
purloined enough weaponry and ammo to
start a small war. And
Cartwright?...

        (London looks at Cartwright,
        who is stuffing his face with
        a large slice of ham.)

...I trust the food and drink is to
your satisfaction?

                    CARTWRIGHT
Yes. It is very good, thank you.
After a good night's sleep and a
glass of warm milk I will be ready
for action.

                    LONDON
That's the ticket, but if I can keep
your attention for a little while
longer, we can all get a few hours
kip before we leave...

        (London pulls out a NR-40
        army knife and runs it along
        a line on the map.)

...This is where are at the
moment, Nikoslava street, and this
point up here, marked with a red

train, is our destination, the
Lengrasky Railway Station.

                    CARTER
And how do you propose we are going
to get there?

                    LONDON
Well, as I said before, we'll wait
for the cover of nightfall and
covertly make our way to the Station.

                    CAVENDISH
We haven't been very covert so far. I
don't think you know the meaning of
the word.

                    LONDON
I wondered how long it would take
before the old Cavendish was back. I
just didn't think it would take one
beer.

                    WINSLOW
Listen, what's that noise?

        (Outside on the street, a
        platoon of Russian soldiers
        and two men wearing nothing
        but their underwear are
        waving Winslow's discarded
        tunic under the nose of three

*Alsatian dogs. After
smelling the tunic, the dogs
rush towards the pawnbrokers
shop.)*

LONDON
Carter, go and see what's happening.

*(Carter goes to the shop
front and looks out through
the barricade. Outside, the
three Alsatians have stopped
at the pawnbrokers and are
barking incessantly and
scratching at the door.
Russian soldiers begin
removing debris from the shop
entrance and Carter returns
to the back of the shop to
inform everyone.)*

CARTER
We've been rumbled! They're coming
in.

LONDON
Quick everyone, out the back!

*(London gathers his map and
they all scramble towards the
back door. Winslow opens it
and is met with a platoon of
Russian soldiers smoking
cigarettes and sheltering*

*from the rain. He closes the
door quickly and bolts it.)*

WINSLOW
We can't go that way.

LONDON
Why, whatever's the matter?

*(The sound of rifle fire is
heard and bullet holes appear
around the backdoor lock.)*

WINSLOW
Soldiers!

LONDON
Quick, back inside. Find anything to
make a barricade...

*(London and his men, start
throwing shelves, pans,
books, T.V.'s, guitars and
anything they can find
against the back door.)*

...Carter, Pilky, get to the front
and hold them off!

*(Carter and Pilkington go to
the front of the shop. The
soldiers begin to enter and
Carter starts firing. The
Russians start shooting, but*

quickly retreat back outside
to the street.)

CARTER
C'mon, where are you going? Come and
get it!...

(Carter keeps his finger on
the trigger of his rifle and
shots blast out the front of
the shop. Pilkington fumbles
with the bolt on his rifle
and it falls out onto the
floor.)

...Where are you going, come back and
fight!

(At the back of the shop,
London, Winslow, Cartwright
and Cavendish continue to
make a barricade.)

LONDON
That should hold them for a while.
Let's go and help Carter and Pilky.

(They go to the front of the
shop to join Carter and
Pilkington. When they get
there, three smoke bombs and
two flashbangs are thrown in
from the outside and land on
the floor.)

CAVENDISH
Cover your ears!

(The flashbangs explode and
the room begins to fill with
smoke. London falls against
a door that leads to the
basement of the shop.)

LONDON
Quickly, everyone into the basement!

(London and his men run down
some stairs into the shop's
basement. At the bottom of
the stairs, there is a thick
metal door. They go through
the door and bolt it shut
from the inside. London
grabs a torch from his pocket
and turns it on. The
basement is dusty with a few
old crates, beds and
blankets.)

PILKINGTON
That's a thick door, they won't get
through that in a hurry.

CAVENDISH
What happens when they do?

                    LONDON
We shall have to fight them off.
Make a stand.

                  CAVENDISH
Like Custer?

                    LONDON
I don't think it will be quite like
the *battle of little big horn*, but we
shall put on a show. We have guns
and ammo, we'll fight for as long as
we can. It's better to go out in a
blaze of glory then be hanged as a
spy.

        *(Gun shots hit the metal door
        but they do not penetrate.
        Russian voices and loud
        banging continue for five
        minutes then silence. A few
        moments later, the sound of
        floorboards being removed can
        be heard.)*

                    CARTER
Listen! What's that?

                  WINSLOW
They're coming in through the
ceiling.

                    LONDON
The dirty rotters. Not very

sportsman like I must say.

(Pilkington sits down on a crate and puts his back against the wall.)

PILKINGTON
Can you hear that?

LONDON
Yes, they are taking up the floor.

PILKINGTON
No, I can hear water. Listen!

CARTER
He's right, I can hear it too.

CARTWRIGHT
It's coming from behind Pilky.

LONDON
Pilky, get off that crate a moment

(Pilkington moves from the crate.)

CARTWRIGHT
Look, underneath the crate, it's a trapdoor!

(London moves the crate out of the way and opens a door

*to reveal a staircase leading
down. Above them, the sound
of Russian soldiers shouting
and floorboards being removed
continues.)*

LONDON
Quickly everyone, it's a way out...

*(London looks around the
basement and notices some old
beds and blankets.)*

...Grab those old beds and blankets.
We can pull them over the top of the
door on the way out. That should buy
us a few more minutes.

*(London and his men descend
into the staircase. Winslow
pulls the beds and blankets
towards him and lets them
fall on the door as it
closes.*

CAVENDISH
I hope this goes somewhere London.

LONDON
You can always go back up to the
basement and hold the Russians off
for a while. You'll get no
complaints from me.

                    CAVENDISH
You'd like that wouldn't you.
Anything to save yourself.

                    LONDON
Oh, shut up Cavendish. You really
are quite annoying.

          *(London and his men arrive at
          the bottom of the staircase
          and exit through an old
          wooden door. The door opens
          into the city sewer and they
          are met with the sweet smell
          of the underworld. Around
          them hundreds of boxes are
          stacked next to the exit
          door.)*

                    WINSLOW
Phoo-wee, it really stinks down here.

                    LONDON
Don't complain too much Winslow,
that's the sweet smell of freedom.

                    CARTER
I wonder what's in all these boxes...

          *(Carter puts on a torch,
          opens a box and shines it
          inside.)*

...It's tinned meat.

*(Cartwright strikes a match
and opens a box.)*

CARTWRIGHT
This one's filled with tins of soup.

(Carter opens another box.)

CARTER
This box has got tins of caviar.

WINSLOW
But what's it all doing here?

LONDON
Must be black market food. The chap
that owns that pawnbroker shop must
be trading in stolen goods. Food is
hard to come by these days. I mean,
look at that chap's fridge, it was
full to the gunnels. Not many
fridges see that amount of food these
days...

*(London shines his torch
along the sewer and checks
his map.)*

...Well, I suppose we better get
going. Grab as much food as you can,
and Cartwright?

CARTWRIGHT
Yes?

LONDON
Make sure you fill your pockets,
don't want you complaining you're
hungry all the time, I have enough
trouble from Cavendish without you
whingeing as well...

> (They all take some food from
> the boxes and fill their
> pockets. London checks his
> map again and looks down the
> tunnel.

...If I'm reading this map right, the
station should be in this direction.

> (They all start to follow
> London.)

...No, sorry, it's this way.

> (London turns around and
> starts to walk in the
> opposite direction. They all
> follow. Winslow moves closer
> to Cavendish and whispers.)

WINSLOW
I hope we are going in the right
direction. I would have said the
Station was north-east from here not
south.

                    CAVENDISH
Why don't you go and tell him.   See
what he says.

        *(London looks at his map
        again.)*

                    LONDON
Sorry chaps, we need to go back the
other way.   I've got it this time.

        *(Winslow and Cavendish look
        at one another and smile.)*

Scene fades.

ACT 1, SCENE 8

3.47pm. Saturday 18th October 2025, 'The Dragon's Breath' public house, Flat 1A, Moscow. Dmitry and Yuri have broken into an upstairs flat above the pub. They have taken several bottles of alcohol and numerous cartons of cigarettes and are relaxing on a large sofa in the lounge. The flat is nicely furnished with a newly fitted black ash style kitchen and light pine dining room set with a rhombus shaped table. In the lounge, a three piece suite sits around a glass coffee table and opposite a big television. The view out of the window looks down on to a main thoroughfare and gives good visibility for approaching traffic. Dmitry picks up a large glass of vodka and takes a drink.

                    DMITRY
That is better. The world seems
great again.

                    YURI
Dmitry, you are a drunk. What do you
mean the world seems great again?

                    DMITRY
Yuri, the world is always better with
Vodka. It is a fact. Just ask
yourself this question. Is the world

better with a cigarette or worse?

                    YURI
It is better of course.

                    DMITRY
Exactly. For you it is cigarettes,
for me, it is vodka...

        (Dmitry takes another drink.)

...It is good we have found our
calling.

                    YURI
I wouldn't exactly call it a calling,
more of a dependency that is crucial
to our wellbeing.

                    DMITRY
Yuri, that is just semantics.
However you look on it, we both feel
better.

        (The sound of army trucks and
        voices can be heard out on
        the street.)

                    YURI
Dmitry, what is that?

                    DMITRY
Sounds like army trucks. I will have

a look...

> (*Dmitry stumbles over to the*
> *window and peers through the*
> *blinds.*)

...It is army trucks alright and a
platoon of soldiers. They are
climbing into the back of the trucks.

                    YURI
Are they leaving?

                    DMITRY
It looks like it. It is really
coming down out there. The road is
like a river. They all look soaked.

                    YURI
Perhaps they are going home.

                    DMITRY
I don't think they will be going
home, but they will be going back to
their camp for a meal and dry
clothes.

                    YURI
That is good news, Dmitry. I hope it
rains for days.

> (*Dmitry walks away from the*
> *window.*)

DMITRY
It will certainly give us a little
breathing space for tonight, but they
will be back tomorrow when it has
stopped raining.

YURI
That is good, I am quite comfortable
on this sofa. I think I will have a
good sleep for a few hours while you
come up with a plan.

(Yuri starts to yawn.)

DMITRY
How many plans must I come up with?

YURI
I am sure you will think of something
while I am asleep.

DMITRY
Perhaps I will sleep too.

YURI
That is good, you should sleep.
Perhaps you will dream up a plan for
us.

DMITRY
I am glad to see you are not
disheartened by our present
situation.

YURI

We've been in tougher spots than
this. I know you will think of
something, you always do.

DMITRY

Well, I thank you for your vote of
confidence. I hope I can live up to
your expectations.

>   *(Yuri falls asleep and Dmitry*
>   *covers him with a blanket.*
>   *Dmitry takes off his shoes,*
>   *pours another drink and sits*
>   *back in a chair. Shortly*
>   *afterwards he is also*
>   *asleep.)*

Scene fades.

ACT 2, SCENE 1

4.11pm. Saturday 18th October 2025, Moscow State University, Moscow. Professor Tromansky has just returned from a late lunch at his local golf club and is making his way into his office at the university. Professor Tromansky is a thin, tall man with a large, gunslinger moustache. He is wearing a Fair Isle pullover, Plus Fours, Argyle socks and a flat cap. He is a resident of Russia, but originally hails from Transylvania in Central Romania. In his right hand, he is carrying a golf club, a 5 iron. In the reception area he speaks to his assistant, Natasha.

PROFESSOR TROMANSKY
Afternoon Natasha, how are things?

NATASHA
We have no power and it seems we are under attack by alien forces.

PROFESSOR TROMANSKY
That is a good one, Natasha. You are quite a quick witted girl.

NATASHA
No, seriously. Where have you been all day?

                    PROFESSOR TROMANSKY
Can't you tell by my attire?

          *(The Professor twirls
          around.)*

                    NATASHA
Let me guess. The circus?

                    PROFESSOR TROMANSKY
Again with the quick wit...

          *(The professor puts down his
          golf club.)*

...Now, has there been any mail?

                    NATASHA
Just a postcard from your Nephew
Dacian. He is somewhere in France on
holiday with his family enjoying the
weather and the outside cooking.
There is a picture of them on the
front porch of a cabin having a
barbeque.

          *(Natasha hands him the
          postcard and he holds it in
          his hand.)*

                    PROFESSOR TROMANSKY
I will read it later, just in case
you have missed something. Is there
anything else.

                    NATASHA
Erm, I don't think so. No, wait.
There are two agents from the KGB in
your office waiting to see you.

              PROFESSOR TROMANSKY
KGB, what do they want?

                    NATASHA
I couldn't say. They've been waiting
for some time. I actually forgot
they were there.

              PROFESSOR TROMANSKY
I must go and see them at once...

        (Professor Tromansky takes
        off his cap and straightens
        his pullover.)

...Remind me to give you a raise.

                    NATASHA
Really?

              PROFESSOR TROMANSKY
No!...

        (The Professor enters his
        office and two KGB agents,
        dressed in black, are
        standing by the window
        smoking cigarettes.)

...Gentleman, sorry to keep you waiting. My assistant didn't inform me of your presence.

> (The agents toss their cigarettes out of the window.)

AGENT STANOVICH
I'm agent Stanovich and this is my partner, agent Ollieov...

> (They all shake hands.)

...I take it you are aware of the recent attack on our nation by alien forces.

PROFESSOR TROMANSKY
Yes, yes, of course.

> (The Professor twiddles his index finger on the desk next to him.)

AGENT STANOVICH
Good. Professor, we need your help.

PROFESSOR TROMANSKY
My help, I can't imagine what I could do for you?

AGENT OLLIEOV
You are a specialist in photographic

analysis and long-wave spectral
anomalies?

PROFESSOR TROMANSKY
Yes. Do you have something you wish
me to look at?

*(Agent Stanovich pulls out a
photograph and hands it to
the Professor. The Professor
takes it with his left hand
placing it over his Nephew's
postcard in his right. He
studies the picture.)*

AGENT STANOVICH
This photograph was taken earlier
today by a local reporter. As you
can see there are some figures in
this picture that are a little
blurry. We were hoping you could
enhance the image so their identity
could be ascertained.

PROFESSOR TROMANSKY
Yes, certainly...

*(The Professor walks over to
a large box and places the
image inside it along with
his Nephew's postcard. He
walks over to a 12 volt
battery and connects the*

cables to the terminals. A
metal machine on his desk
begins to whirr.)

...This machine is a little
temperamental, but it should do the
trick. I can't use the bigger
enlarger without power, but this has
never let me down...

(An image appears on the wall
on the other side of the
office. It is blurry at
first, but then after a few
adjustments and twiddling of
knobs by the Professor, the
image becomes clear.)

...Yes, that should do it.

(The two agents and the
Professor study the image
which shows Dmitry, Yuri,
Kal, MacTavish, London and
his group of Ex-SAS soldiers
climbing out of the Red Neval
spaceship.)

                AGENT STANOVICH
That is much clearer already. Do you
think you can isolate the figures to
give us a clearer image of their
faces?

PROFESSOR TROMANSKY
Yes, I should be able to enhance the
facial features and give you a print
out.

AGENT OLLIEOV
Very good.

*(Moments later, a group of
6x4 pictures drop out of a
metal tray attached to the
Professor's machine. He
hands them to agent
Stanovich.)*

AGENT STANOVICH
Excellent. There is no doubt about
it. This is definitely Dmitry Usakov
and Yuri Chekov.

PROFESSOR TROMANSKY
I thought they were dead. Blew
themselves up if I remember correctly
on the I.S.S. How can they be in
this picture?

AGENT OLLIEOV
We shall have to let the President
know as soon as possible.

AGENT STANOVICH
What about the others?

AGENT OLLIEOV
We shall have to put out an alert and
inform the press. For now, we can
show their faces and say they are
wanted for questioning.

(Agent Stanovich looks
towards the Professor.)

AGENT STANOVICH
Professor, can you extrapolate any
other information from the
photograph?

PROFESSOR TROMANSKY
Yes, I can run it through an infrared
filter to see if there is anything
hidden within the image.

AGENT STANOVICH
Could you do that, please?

PROFESSOR TROMANSKY
Certainly...

(The Professor turns a few
dials and flicks a few knobs.
A strange whistling sound
followed by a low hum comes
from his machine and an image
starts to emerge from within
the photo. Orange, blue, red
and yellow forms dance on the
wall and a disturbing image

appears.)

...Well, I wasn't expecting that.

                    AGENT STANOVICH
What do you make of it Professor?

                    PROFESSOR TROMANSKY
It would seem that the two figures in
the front, the one's you believed to
be Dmitry Usakov and Yuri Chekov have
little people inside them. It looks
like a boy and a girl. I must say,
their faces look familiar. And the
rest of the image is quite strange,
looks like a barbeque of some sorts.

                    AGENT STANOVICH
What does it mean?

                    PROFESSOR TROMANSKY
Well, it can only mean one thing.
There are aliens living inside of
these people. It's that or they have
been cloned.

                    AGENT OLLIEOV
Is that possible?

                    PROFESSOR TROMANSKY
Not on this planet, but on others
certainly. I shall have to do a bit
more research, but I should be able

to give you a full report later today.

                    AGENT STANOVICH
Well, thank you very much Professor Tromansky. We must be going now. The President needs to be informed.

        (They all shake hands.)

                    PROFESSOR TROMANSKY
Yes, well, give him my regards. My assistant, Natasha, at the reception will give you my contact details.

                    AGENT STANOVICH
Thank you very much Professor.

        (Agent Stanovich and Ollieov leave the Professor's office. The Professor looks at the image on the wall.)

                    PROFESSOR TROMANSKY
Can't help thinking I've seen those faces before...

        (The Professor looks out of the window and waves goodbye to Agents Stanovich and Ollieov.)

...Now, I think a nice afternoon cocktail is in order...

*(He rubs his hands together
and grabs a glass beaker from
a cupboard and fills it to
the first mark with vodka.)*

...Now, where did I put the ginger
beer and the mint.

Scene fades.

ACT 2, SCENE 2

4.27pm. Saturday 18th October 2025, The sewers, Moscow. London and his team of ex-SAS soldiers have been wondering around in the sewers for the past 45 minutes. They have reached a fork in the tunnel that branches off into two different sections and have stopped to ponder their course of action. Around them, rats scurry and swim about searching for dry land as the water level continues to rise.

LONDON
Well, according to this map, we must be nearly there, but it doesn't say anything about this tunnel splitting into a fork.

CAVENDISH
Why would a map of a railway line show you the layout of a sewer?

LONDON
Aah! Yes, well, maybe that's where I've been going wrong. Didn't think about that.

> (In the distance, a rumble
> followed by a clang and a
> thump is heard then the sound
> of a train breaking hard.)

PILKINGTON
That sounds like a train stopping.

LONDON
We must be near the Station, that
sounded like a points change over to
me.

CAVENDISH
So, you know the sound of a points
change over but you can't read a map.

LONDON
For your information Cavendish, I
once lived next to Kings Cross
Station. On my way to work, the
points were changed over at 8.23am
everyday for the train arriving from
Kettering. It sounded just like
that. A clang followed by a thump.

CARTER
It sounds like it's coming from this
direction. I'll go and have a quick
look.

        (Carter wanders off down the
        right channel and Pilkington
        and Winslow appear from
        behind.)

WINSLOW
Are we there yet? I'm getting
awfully wet.

*(London turns around to look
at Winslow and Pilkington.)*

LONDON
Where have you two been?

PILKINGTON
Winslow lost his crystals, so we went
back to look for them.

LONDON
What?

WINSLOW
You know, the magic green crystals.

LONDON
The one's we've been risking our
lives for, those green crystals?

WINSLOW
Yes, but it's not my fault, it's all
this running around in dark places.

CAVENDISH
When did you last have them?

WINSLOW
I was just saying to Pilkington that
I remember having them at the clothes
shop.

(Carter reappears from the

tunnel ahead.)

                    CARTER
Come on it's this way.   I've found an
exit.

                    LONDON
Just a minute Carter.   Winslow's lost
the crystals.

                    WINSLOW
Well don't say it like that, I didn't
do it on purpose.

                    CARTER
Did you take them out of your tunic
when you changed over your clothes at
the florists?

    (Winslow's face turns red.)

                    WINSLOW
Oh!

                    LONDON
Oh!   What does that mean?

                    WINSLOW
Carter's right, I forgot all about
that.

                    LONDON
You fool Winslow.

                    WINSLOW
I'm sorry, I'll go back and get
them.

                    CARTER
That's no good, they're gone.

                    LONDON
How do you know that Carter?

                    CARTER
Because the Russian soldiers we've
been running from for the last hour
had Winslow's tunic stuffed under the
nose of those Alsatian dogs getting
his scent.

                    LONDON
Maybe they had Pilky's tunic?

                    CARTER
It's possible, let's go and ask them.

                    LONDON
Well, I guess that's that.

                    CAVENDISH
Well, London, what are we doing?

        (The water continues to rise
        in the sewer and starts to
        gush and plop.)

                    LONDON
We are getting out of here. Carter
still has the Medallion, that's the
main thing...

          *(London looks over to
          Carter.)*

...You do still have the Medallion
Carter, you didn't lose it out of a
hole in your pocket or leave it
somewhere?

                    CARTER
No, I've still got it.   It's in the
inside pocket of my tunic.

          *(Carter puts his hand in his
          pocket and retrieves the
          Medallion to show to London.
          He holds it up for everyone
          to see.)*

                    CAVENDISH
I might be seeing things Carter, but
unless that Medallion of yours has
disguised itself as a tin of tuna, I
would say you've lost it.

                    CARTER
What?...

          (Carter examines the tin.)

...I could've sworn I put it in that
pocket. Let me check...

(London takes the tin of tuna
from Carter and studies it.
Carter starts to empty his
pockets.)

...It must be here somewhere!

LONDON
Don't bother Carter, you haven't got
it.

CARTER
What?

LONDON
Dmitry and Yuri have it.

CARTER
Don't be silly, Dmitry gave it to me
and I put it in my pocket.

LONDON
Maybe so, but one of them took it
back from you.

CAVENDISH
How do you know that London?

(London looks at the tin of
tuna.)

LONDON
This isn't an ordinary tin of tuna,
it's Russian and is stamped with a
Zitex code. This has come from the
International Space Station. This
stamp on the side of the tin says so.
There is only one way you could have
got this tin, Carter.

CARTER
From someone who's just come from the
Space Station.

LONDON
And by process of elimination, we
arrive at Dmitry and Yuri.

CARTER
Those bleedin' rats, I'll kill 'em!

*(Lights start to flash along
the tunnel walls and Russian
soldiers can be heard
advancing on their position.)*

CARTWRIGHT
The Russians, they're here!

*(Shots ring out and bounce
off the tunnel walls.)*

CAVENDISH
London, c'mon. We've got to get out
of here!

(London and his team of ex-SAS soldiers wade through the water as fast as they can. The level continues to rise and is now at chest height. Ahead, a ladder leads out of the sewer to the street above.)

LONDON
C'mon chaps, almost there...

(They arrive at a metal ladder leading to a manhole cover above.)

...Cavendish, you go first. We'll need a good strong chap to open that lid...

(Cavendish and Pilkington start climbing the ladder. Carter, Winslow and Cartwright fire at the advancing Russians and cling to the tunnel walls.)

...C'mon, we've got to leave...

(London holds on tight to the bottom of the ladder and starts to climb up quickly when a huge surge of water explodes down the tunnel. Carter, Winslow and

Cartwright are swept away
with the sudden surge and
disappear out of sight
towards the advancing Russian
soldiers.)

...Carter!

(London starts to climbs up
the ladder. Cavendish and
Pilkington are at the top and
are waiting for the others
before they pop the lid.
Pilkington looks down the
ladder.)

                    PILKINGTON
Where are the others?

                    LONDON
They're gone.

                    PILKINGTON
What do you mean gone?

                    LONDON
They were washed away.

(Cavendish pushes opens the
lid. In front of him he can
see Russian soldiers and the
train station courtyard.
It's raining hard and
slightly misty. Visibility

is poor and the daylight is
fading.)

LONDON
What can you see Cavendish?

CAVENDISH
It's the train station courtyard.
There are Russian soldiers on patrol
and a chap 10 feet away. I will take
care of him, and then come back for
you...

(*Cavendish looks down the*
ladder.)

...Where are the others?

PILKINGTON
Gone.

(*Cavendish puts his head down*
for a moment.)

CAVENDISH
I'll go out and take care of this
guy, wait here...

(*Cavendish pushes the manhole*
cover to one side and
stealthily walks across the
waterlogged, gravelled
courtyard and creeps up
behind the Russian soldier.

He takes out his knife and
slits his throat. He drags
the body out of the way and
covers it with a nearby
tarpaulin. The rain turns to
sleet and the wind starts to
blow.)

...Okay, it's clear, you can come out
now.

(London and Pilkington climb
out of the hole and join
Cavendish by a pile of
railway sleepers.)

CAVENDISH
What happened to the others, were
they shot?

LONDON
No, they got carried away in the
water. They must of opened up the
sluice gates somewhere.

CAVENDISH
That's how Carter's grandfather died.

LONDON
Really, what an odd coincidence.
It's a tough break for us, Carter was
a good man in a tight spot. When
this is over, I think we shall go and
have a word with those chaps at the

water plant. Opening the sluice
gates like that, they should be
sacked.

                  PILKINGTON
I don't suppose they thought anyone
would be down in the sewer.

                  LONDON
All the same Pilky, they're a rotten
lot who deserve a jolly good
thrashing.

        (Cavendish looks around for
        enemy soldiers and turns back
        to London.)

                  CAVENDISH
What are we going to do now with just
three of us?

                  LONDON
Glory on, it's the only thing to do.
There's only ten more minutes of
daylight before it's totally dark, so
I suggest we scope this place out a
bit with the old binoculars and see
if we can find a way in to the
Station Master's office.

        (Over by the manhole cover,
        an arm pops out of the hole.)

PILKINGTON
Look! Someone's coming out of the
hole.

(London aims his pistol at
the hole.)

LONDON
Hope it's not the Russians. Go and
have a look Cavendish.

(Cavendish goes over to the
hole and pulls out three
bedraggled bodies onto the
gravel.)

CAVENDISH
It's Carter, Winslow and Cartwright.
Give me a hand.

(London and Pilkington walk
over to Cavendish. They grab
Cartwright and Winslow and
Cavendish gets Carter. They
all walk back to the pile of
railway sleepers and collapse
in a heap.)

LONDON
We thought we'd lost you.

CARTER
You can't get rid of us that easy,
London.

(Carter is shivering violently and his teeth are chattering.)

                    LONDON
Well, we better get somewhere so we
can dry your clothes. The
temperature's going to drop and
you'll freeze to death.

*(Cavendish scopes out the
area with a pair of
binoculars and spies the
railway station platform to
the north of their position
and a signalman's box to the
east.)*

                  CAVENDISH
I can see the Station Master's office
and the railway platform. It looks
pretty busy with soldiers on patrol
and waiting passengers...

*(Cavendish moves his
position.)*

...There's a signalman's box down the
track about a 150 yards away, east of
our position. That's bound to be
warm and there'll only be one guy to
deal with.

LONDON
Sounds good Cavendish, lead the way.

*(Darkness falls and London
and his group of ex-SAS
soldiers make their way
towards the signal box. The
sleet turns to snow and gives
them excellent cover to walk
down the track unnoticed. A
light is on inside the signal
box and a lone man wanders
back and forth carrying a cup
of tea and smoking a pipe.)*

PILKINGTON
There's a chap inside.

LONDON
Yes, I can see that Pilky. Looks
like he has tea.

CAVENDISH
Leave this to me.

LONDON
Good show Cavendish. See if you can
just knock him out and tie him up. I
don't think we should be killing any
innocent civilians unnecessarily,
it's bad for the old curriculum
vitae.

                    CAVENDISH
I'll do my best.

    *(Cavendish creeps towards the
    signal box while the others
    look on. He enters, grabs
    the signalman from behind and
    hits him over the head with
    the butt of his gun. The man
    falls unconscious and
    Cavendish carries him outside
    and dumps him in the bushes.
    He gags him and ties his
    wrists and feet with some
    twine. He looks around, and
    then returns to the others.)*

                    LONDON
Good show Cavendish. Right, let's
get in the warm...

    *(London and his team of ex-
    SAS soldiers enter the signal
    box and huddle around a cast
    iron stove.)*

                    WINSLOW
I can feel me fingers again.

                    LONDON
It's Probably best if we all strip
off and hang out our clothes to
dry...

*(They begin to undress down
to their underwear.)*

...Look, we can hang our clothes on
these tall levers sticking up from
the floor. They should get quite a
good airing on those.

*(Pilkington notices a kettle
on the side and picks it up.)*

PILKINGTON
Shall I put the kettle on?

LONDON
Sounds like an excellent idea, Pilky.
I bet we could all do with a nice cup
of tea.

CARTER
Sounds like heaven.

LONDON
Glad we're not outside on that track
anymore, wind's picked up something
fierce and it's a complete
whiteout...

*(London warms himself by the
stove.)*

...At least all this snow has
provided us with excellent cover.
Shouldn't think anyone will be out in

this.

> *(Winslow opens a cupboard and pulls out a small white packet and a bottle of brandy. London looks to see what Winslow has in his hands.)*

...What have you got there Winslow?

                    WINSLOW
A bottle of brandy and a packet that says 'Pikelets'.

                    LONDON
Pikelets? I say, things really are looking up. Who would of thought that a signalman would have had a packet of Pikelets. Must be a fellow of good breeding and clarity of thought. Shame we had to knock him out and leave him in the snow...

> *(London hands Cavendish a grey woollen blanket from a shelf.)*

...Go and put this blanket over that fellow you knocked out, it's the least we can do if we are going to eat his Pikelets and drink his tea.

                    CAVENDISH
Are you mad?

                     LONDON
The thought wouldn't have even
crossed my mind if he'd left us with
a packet of Jaffa cakes, but
Pikelets?   It's the decent thing to
do.

Scene fades.

ACT 2, SCENE 3

11.08am. Thursday 30th January 1986, Dalnegorsk, Russia. Colonel P. Chekov has returned to his tent at the base camp and is waiting for General Spuriovsky to arrive. On the side of the Izvestkovaya mountain, local workers from the nearby lead mine are carrying what looks like to be a large lump of coal. Local wives and children are skipping down the side of the mountain and singing songs. Colonel P. Chekov and Jnr. Sgt. Smithsky are playing a game of darts when they hear the commotion.

COLONEL P. CHEKOV
Smithsky, Go and see what is happening outside.

JNR. SGT. SMITHSKY
Right away Colonel.

(Jnr. Sgt. Smithsky goes outside and runs up to a local man who is helping to carry a large lump of coal. After a short conversation, he returns to the colonel.)

COLONEL P. CHEKOV
Well, did you find out what the disturbance was?

JNR. SGT. SMITHSKY
I think you better come and look.

*(Colonel Chekov goes outside
and looks at the parade of
people walking past.)*

COLONEL P. CHEKOV
Who are all these people?

JNR. SGT. SMITHSKY
They are workers from the local lead
mine.

COLONEL P. CHEKOV
What are they doing here?

JNR. SGT. SMITHSKY
They are celebrating.

COLONEL P. CHEKOV
Celebrating, what is there to
celebrate about? And what's that
they are carrying?

JNR. SGT. SMITHSKY
They have found a large lump of coal.
They say it is a good sign. They are
taking the coal to be weighed in the
village and they have sent for the
man from the *Guinness Book of
Records.*

COLONEL CHEKOV
Where did they find it exactly?

JNR. SGT. SMITHSKY
On the side of the mountain, not far
from where the alien was found.

(A helicopter carrying
General Spuriovsky lands at
the camp. The General gets
out and walks over to the
Colonel and the Jnr. Sgt. He
looks angry. The parade of
people continue to walk past
singing and waving.)

GENERAL SPURIOVSKY
Colonel. What's going on here? And
what are all these people doing in
this area? Don't you know this
whole region has been placed under
quarantine? Why haven't you cordoned
off the area and put up a fence?
Where is the road blockade and the
sentry box guard? More to the point,
where's your platoon?

COLONEL P. CHEKOV
I think most of them are still eating
lunch and the rest are on the hill.

GENERAL SPURIOVSKY
Lunch! It's only 11am. Get them out
here at once.

COLONEL P. CHEKOV
Right away General...

*(The Colonel salutes the
General and walks over to the
mess tent.)*

...Everybody out on the double.

*(The platoon slowly exits the
mess tent. Some are still
carrying bits of food and
others have open bottles of
beer.)*

...Attention!

*(The platoon barely stand up
straight and look slovenly.
General Spuriovsky walks over
and looks at the men then
addresses the Colonel.)*

GENERAL SPURIOVSKY
Why aren't these men dressed
properly?...

*(The General walks over to a
Private who is leaning
against another soldier.)*

...You there, stand to attention.

(The Private puts his feet

together and falls over. A
beer bottle slips out of his
tunic and breaks on the
ground.)

...Colonel, this man is drunk.

COLONEL P. CHEKOV
Yes, sir.

GENERAL SPURIOVSKY
What do you mean, yes, sir? This man
is a disgrace to the motherland, and
the others don't look much better...

(The General looks at Colonel
Chekov and notices something
strange about his attire.)

...Colonel, are those pyjamas under
your tunic?

COLONEL P. CHEKOV
Yes, it was cold this morning and I
had left my thermals at home.

GENERAL SPURIOVSKY
Colonel. It is clear to me that not
only have you given up, but so has
your platoon. As of now, you are
relieved of duty. You have failed to
carry out the simplest of orders and
command a platoon to a satisfactory
level. Unfortunately, when I return

to head quarters, I will have no
alternative but to make a full report
on what I have seen here today and
make a recommendation that you should
be demoted to the rank of Private and
be put on simple kitchen duties.

                COLONEL P. CHEKOV
Demoted again. Last year, I was a
General just like you. You can't do
this, it's not right.

            (The General turns to Jnr.
            Sgt. Smithsky.)

                GENERAL SPURIOVSKY
What is your name Jnr. Sgt.?

                JNR. SGT. SMITHSKY
Smithsky, sir.

                GENERAL SPURIOVSKY
You've now been promoted to acting
Sgt. Smithsky. If you can get these
men into shape by the end of the
week, we will make it official.

                JNR. SGT. SMITHSKY
Thank you, sir. I will do my best.

                GENERAL SPURIOVSKY
Now, Colonel. Escort me to your tent
and give me a full report. If you

manage to do that, perhaps you'll get
to keep the rank of Corporal.

*(The Colonel and the General
walk over to the base camp
tent and walk inside.)*

GENERAL SPURIOVSKY
What's all this, card tables,
dartboards, women's brassiere
catalogues!...

*(The General looks around the
tent.)*

...What are all these open boxes of
food doing in here, and what's in
that body bag?

COLONEL P. CHEKOV
That is the alien, sir.

GENERAL SPURIOVSKY
The alien?

COLONEL P. CHEKOV
Yes, the one we took down from the
mountain.

GENERAL SPURIOVSKY
Why wasn't I informed of this?

COLONEL P. CHEKOV
We only found him moments before you
arrived.

GENERAL SPURIOVSKY
Have you contacted Major Finkonsky at
the 103rd Army base in Venchsnech?

COLONEL P. CHEKOV
No, not yet.

GENERAL SPURIOVSKY
Then do it at once. We must preserve
the body as best we can. Tell him to
get a team together as soon as
possible.

COLONEL P. CHEKOV
Yes, sir. I will do it right away.

*(The Colonel walks over to
the radio set and starts
turning the dials and the
General unzips the body bag.)*

GENERAL SPURIOVSKY
Did you find anything on the alien?
Any flight plans, weapons or advanced
machinery?

COLONEL P. CHEKOV
No, nothing.

(*Jnr. Sgt. Smithsky enters the tent and addresses the General*)

JNR. SGT. SMITHSKY
Sir. The area is now cordoned off and an electric fence has been erected. The road blockade is in operation and a guard is posted at the sentry box.

GENERAL SPURIOVSKY
Very good Sergeant. Carry on.

JNR. SGT. SMITHSKY
Yes, sir.

(*Jnr. Sgt. Smithsky leaves the tent. The Colonel is still trying to get the radio to work.*)

GENERAL SPURIOVSKY
What are you doing with that radio Colonel?

COLONEL P. CHEKOV
Seems to be broken.

(*The General walks over to the radio, flips a switch and it turns on.*)

GENERAL SPURIOVSKY
Go and get me a cup of coffee. I
will see to this myself.

COLONEL P. CHEKOV
Very good, sir.

*(The Colonel leaves to get
the General a coffee.)*

GENERAL SPURIOVSKY
What an idiot!

Scene fades.

ACT 2, SCENE 4

6.17pm. Saturday 18th October 2025, Lengrasky railway yard, Moscow. Inside the signal box, London and his team of ex-SAS soldiers gather round a cast iron stove for heat. For the past 48 minutes and 7 seconds, their clothes have been drying over the point and signal control levers for the railway line and they are almost dry. Outside, the snow has continued to cover the tracks and visibility is limited. Russian soldiers on guard at the station, have gathered around a fire contained in an old oil drum to keep warm. They talk, smoke, and stamp their feet in the snow.

LONDON
I don't know about you chaps, but I'm feeling much better after those Pikelets...

*(London rubs his hands
together and smiles.)*

...and that brand of tea was quite superior to the usual dishwater I get served up at the local cricket club.

CARTWRIGHT
You don't think it was the dash of brandy that gave it a pleasing taste?

*(London paces around the room
glancing out of the windows.)*

LONDON
I have to confess, the brandy was a
welcome addition after the wet and
the cold, but I don't think it was
that. The quality of the tea and
particular blend were quite
exceptional. I have a feeling our
friend outside in the cold might have
been a person of worth. Somebody who
appreciates the good things in life.
It's a shame we've had to be so
ghastly. Perhaps when we get home, I
can send him a food coupon or
something to make up for the food and
drink we've taken.

CARTER
Yeh, and I'll have a whip round at
the local pub.

LONDON
Would you do that Carter?...

*(Carter looks up at London
with raised eyebrows.)*

...Oh, I see. You mock me. Yes,
well all the same...

*(London breaks from his
monologue when he notices a*

light flashing on the signal
and points control panel.)

...How long has that light been
flashing?

                    CARTWRIGHT
What light?

                    LONDON
The one behind your head on that
control board thingy.

          (Cavendish moves from the
          stove.)

                    CAVENDISH
There's a train coming.

                    WINSLOW
A train? I like trains, especially
ones with steam.

                    LONDON
What does it mean exactly?

                    CAVENDISH
I thought you were the expert on
railway points.

                    LONDON
Who me? Not a bit, I just know what
they sound like when they are

changed, that's all.

                    CARTWRIGHT
What do we do?

                    LONDON
Well, let's pull a few levers and see
what happens.

                    CARTER
Leave it alone. I wouldn't start
messin' around with things you know
nothing about.

                    CAVENDISH
That's never stopped him before.

        (London looks at the control
        board.)

                    LONDON
Look! There are more red lights, and
this section of the track is flashing
the number 47...

        (London studies the lights.)

...They seem to be running into a
siding. It appears to be a dead end.
We must have to change the points to
redirect the train back onto the main
line. Help me get these clothes off
the levers. It's probably best if we
put them back on, we can't stay here

much longer without being discovered.

(London and his team of ex-SAS soldiers start to remove their clothes from the point and signal levers and put them back on. Winslow's coat gets caught in a gear and he tries to pull it free.)

PILKINGTON

I can hear a train...

(The sound of a train gets closer, then flies past the signal box.)

...It's a military train.

LONDON

What?

(London puts his left leg into a pair of trousers, then looks out of the window as the train goes whizzing past. Tanks, helicopters, trucks, jeeps, cannons and carriages of Russian soldiers fly by with a familiar clickety-clack.)

WINSLOW

My coat's caught in the gear.

*(London quickly gets dressed
then looks at the levers and
finds number 47. Winslow is
tugging at his coat at lever
47.)*

LONDON

Oh, dear! Cavendish, give me a hand,
Winslow's coat is caught in the gear.

*(Cavendish pulls at the coat
and it rips in two. He falls
on the floor holding half of
the coat.)*

WINSLOW

My coat!

*(The red lights begin
flashing on the control panel
and an alarm sounds. The
train passes the points and
manoeuvres into a siding.)*

LONDON

I think we have more things to worry
about than your coat Winslow!

CARTER

The train's gone into the siding.

CARTWRIGHT
What are we going to do, that train
is going to crash!

(London looks at the control
board.)

LONDON
I think we've got about 20 seconds
before that train crashes and comes
off the track, then this place will
be like a hornet's nest...

(London looks around the room
and takes a bottle of brandy
out of the cupboard.)

...We're in trouble now, it's bad
enough being in a foreign country as
a spy, but this is sabotage.
Derailing a military train full of
weaponry and soldiers is a crime we
don't want to be connected with,
it'll be the firing squad for the lot
of us.

CARTER
This is no time for a drink London,
what the bleedin' hell are we going
to do?

LONDON
It's not for me Carter...

(London looks at Cavendish.)

...Cavendish, go and get that
signalman laying out in the snow and
bring him in here. Make sure you
only leave one set of footprints.

                    CAVENDISH
What for?

                    LONDON
Just do it Cavendish, there's no time
to explain.

        (Cavendish runs outside and
        picks up the signalman and
        brings him back and places
        him down by the stove.)

...Carter, see if you can get that
last piece of Winslow's coat out of
that gear.

        (Carter walks over to the
        gear and starts removing some
        coat fragments. London opens
        the bottle of brandy and
        starts to pour it over the
        signalman's shirt and jacket.
        He lifts his head and pours
        some down his throat.)

                    CAVENDISH
What are you doing London?

        *(A few hundred yards up the
        track, the sound of a train's
        brakes squealing followed by
        metal crunching and a strange
        whoop, whoop, zoom noise
        reverberates around the
        railway yard.)*

                    CARTER
It's crashed.

        *(A tremendous explosion
        lights up the sky, screaming
        and sirens begin to fill the
        air and Russian soldiers run
        down the track to the scene
        of the crash.)*

                    LONDON
Blast. Listen up! We are getting
out of here, but we have to use
Cavendish's footprints. Step only
where he has stepped.

        (Cavendish looks at London.)

                    CAVENDISH
What's going on London?

                    LONDON
This chap...

*(London points and the
unconscious signalman.)*

...is taking the fall. When the army
turn up in the next few minutes, they
will smell the brandy on him and
instantly believe that he is drunk.
They will blame him for the accident
and we will be in the clear. He
doesn't know what happened, or that
we were ever here, he's been knocked
out all this time.

CAVENDISH
Well, what was all that stuff about
him being a decent chap and sending
him a food coupon because you felt
sorry for him?

LONDON
That was then Cavendish, this is now.
When needs must and so forth. Now,
c'mon let's get going, this is an
amazing opportunity to get into that
Station Master's office and contact
H.Q. Couldn't of wished for a better
diversion than this.

*(London and his band of merry
men carefully walk out of the
signal box and run into a
line of bushes along the
station yard fence. They
circumvent some Russian*

soldiers running towards the
crash site and, after
clinging to various train
wheels, timber frames, spare
railway track and small
concrete sheds, they find
themselves outside of a big
red building. A sign above a
door reads: 'Station Master's
Office'. Carter peers inside
a window.)

CARTER
It's clear, there's nobody in there.

LONDON
That train crash was a stroke of
luck, everyone's over there.

(London addresses the group.)

...Carter, Pilky? You come with me.
Cavendish, Cartwright and Winslow -
Stay here and keep look out.

(London, Carter and
Pilkington enter the Station
Master's office.)

CARTER
So, where's this radio?

(London, Carter and
Pilkington look around the

office.)

                    PILKINGTON
It's here on this desk, under this
pile of papers.

                    LONDON
Good show, Pilky.

        (London moves the papers out
        of the way and takes a seat
        at the desk, moves the dial
        on the radio to BROADCOM
        7.9GHS, flips a switch
        reading TRANSMIT and twists a
        knob past LUXEMBURG,
        COPENHAGEN, ZURICH AND
        HELSINKI and stops on
        ENGLAND.)

...This is Red Squirrel calling Tiny
Tim, Over.

        (The radio transmits static.)

...This is Red Squirrel calling Tiny
Tim, Over.

        (A voice is heard.)

                LUCAS B. WINDBAG
This is Tiny Tim. Where are you?
Over.

LONDON
We are in Moscow. Over.

LUCAS B. WINDBAG
What the blazes are you doing there?
What happened to your pick up last
night? We've been expecting your
arrival. Over

LONDON
L.Z. compromised, cherry picker
destroyed. Over.

LUCAS B. WINDBAG
Cherry Picker destroyed, dear, oh
dear. Do you know how much a Cherry
Picker costs?

LONDON
I'm sure they're quite expensive. No
time for small talk. Need immediate
extraction. Over.

LUCAS B. WINDBAG
Extraction impossible. Moscow no fly
zone. Over.

LONDON
Then where? Over.

LUCAS B. WINDBAG
One moment Tiny Tim. Over.

                    CARTER
This doesn't sound good.

                  PILKINGTON
Well, I hope they arrange something
for us, all this running about is
playing havoc with my sciatica.

     *(Static and whistling is
      heard.)*

               LUCAS B. WINDBAG
Extraction set for 18.00 hours
tomorrow night. At the Bolnoy
Children's Hospital in Tiver. Pick
up from main helipad. Over.

                    LONDON
Did you say 'Tiver'? Over.

               LUCAS B. WINDBAG
That's correct. Over.

                    LONDON
That's over a hundred miles away.

               LUCAS B. WINDBAG
Best we can do. Over.

                    LONDON
Okay. Over and out.

CARTER
Tiver, how are we going to get there?

PILKINGTON
Isn't that going back in the
direction of Numenobman lake?

LONDON
Yes, I'm afraid so.

CARTER
So, what's happening now?

(Outside, on the station
platform, a public-address
system can be heard.)

P.A. SYSTEM
...NEXT TRAIN LEAVING FROM PLATFORM 2
IS THE 6.45PM TO TIVER. THIS WILL BE
THE LAST SERVICE OF THE EVENING.
CALLING AT: SECHNOGORSK, KILN,
AVIDOV, OKSHIN, ORODNYA AND MAUS.
THANK YOU...

PILKINGTON
Did you hear that, that train is
going to Tiver.

LONDON
Yes, but it won't do us much good
without a ticket. We can't just go
up to the ticket counter without a

passport or proof of identity. Can't
imagine for a moment they will just
sell me six tickets without asking
for an identity card, especially
after their railway yard has just
been destroyed and curfew's about to
start.

(Pilkington picks up a roll
of unused tickets lying next
to a cap by the door.)

PILKINGTON
What about these?

(London walks over to
Pilkington and examines the
tickets.)

LONDON
First class tickets, and look, the
Station Master's cap.

CARTER
He must have left them there and ran
over to the train wreck.

LONDON
Well, whatever happened it's another
stroke of good fortune for us...

(London tears off six tickets
and puts the roll back next
to the cap.)

...There.   No one will even know we were here; and Cavendish says I can't be covert...

(*London walks over to the door and peers out.*)

...C'mon, let's get back to the others.

(*London, Carter and Pilkington go outside and meet up with Cavendish and Cartwright.*)

LONDON
Where's Winslow.

CAVENDISH
He got cold without his coat and had to go to the bathroom.

LONDON
So, where is he now?

CAVENDISH
He went on the platform to try and find a convenience.

LONDON
Damn it. We've got to leave now.

                    CARTWRIGHT
Where are we going, my leg is
hurting?

                     LONDON
We're going on that train...

          (London points over to the
          railway station platform
          where a diesel train sits
          waiting to depart.)

...We need to get to Tiver for
extraction.

                    CAVENDISH
Tiver, that's going back to where we
came from!

                     LONDON
Look, we haven't got time to chew the
fat just now, that train is leaving
and we need to be on it.

                    CARTWRIGHT
What about tickets?

                     LONDON
It's all been sorted. Now, c'mon,
we've got to find Winslow.

          (On the platform, a railway
          conductor is shouting out,
          'All aboard'. Winslow

*appears from the Gentlemen's
lavatory and meets up with
London and the rest on the
platform. He has acquired a
new overcoat that looks far
too big for him.)*

LONDON
C'mon Winslow, we'd thought we'd lost
you for a moment...

*(They all board the train and
sit in a compartment by
themselves. Cavendish takes
everyone's rifle and places
it under the seat out of
sight.)*

Where did you get that coat from?

WINSLOW
It was hanging on a hook in the
bathroom. I was cold, so I took it.

LONDON
I see. It's a bit big, but beggars
can't be choosers.

(Cavendish leans forward.)

CAVENDISH
So, what's the plan?

LONDON
We've been given an extraction point
for 18.00 hours tomorrow night at the
Bolnoy Children's Hospital in Tiver.
Moscow's too hot just now, so it's
understandable they can't come and
get us here...

(London sits back in his
chair.)

...All we have to do is sit back on
this train and enjoy the ride. When
we get to Tiver, there shouldn't be
any soldiers. They're all in Moscow.

CARTWRIGHT
What about tickets? The train
conductor will be here in a minute.

(London reaches inside his
coat pocket and pulls out six
tickets.)

LONDON
Here, take a ticket.

CAVENDISH
Well, London, you do surprise me.

LONDON
Listen Cavendish, I told you I would
get us out of this mess and if I
don't, I will die trying. Is that

good enough for you?

                    CAVENDISH
Aye, it is.

Scene fades.

ACT 2, SCENE 5

7.11pm Saturday 18th October 2025,
'The Dragon's Breath' public house,
Flat 1A, Moscow. Inside the living
room, Yuri sleeps silently on the
couch. On a shelf above a desk, seven
tea light candles shine brightly where
Dmitry sits writing a letter. He
knocks a book on the floor and Yuri
wakes up.

                    YURI
What! I will have a little black
pepper if you don't mind...

        *(Yuri moves from his lying
        position and sits up. He
        focuses on Dmitry at the
        desk.)*

...Dmitry, you're awake. What time
is it?

                    DMITRY
It is a little after 7pm. Did you
have a good sleep.

                    YURI
Yes, it was very satisfying. I was
having a nice meal at a restaurant:
salmon en croûte, baby asparagus, new
boiled potatoes with garlic butter
and a few oyster mushrooms. The

waiter was about to pour the wine, a
1973 chardonnay, Chateau Montelena.
A very nice wine. Then the fool
slipped and dropped bottle. If I
hadn't woken up, that waiter would
have been in trouble, I would have
got the manager to sack him.

                    DMITRY
I can't offer you 1973 Chateau
Montelena, but I can offer you
coffee.

                    YURI
You have made coffee?

                    DMITRY
I can make coffee.

                    YURI
I thought there was no power?

                    DMITRY
There was old portable gas cooker in
kitchen cupboard with kettle.

                    YURI
Good. I like people who are prepared
for a crisis. It shows they are
organised...

          (Yuri reaches forward and
          grabs a cigarette from a

packet then lights it.)

...That's better.

*(Dmitry walks into the
kitchen then returns with a
coffee for Yuri.)*

                    YURI
Thank you. Are you not having one.

                    DMITRY
No, I have had three already.

(Yuri takes a sip of coffee.)

                    YURI
Not bad. The roast is not quite as
strong as I like, but the flavour is
good...

*(Yuri places his cup on a
coffee table by the couch and
takes a puff from his
cigarette.)*

...I see you are clean and have found
some clothes?

*(Dmitry sits back at the
desk.)*

                    DMITRY
Yes. I had a hot shower, then found

a shirt and a pair of trousers in the owner's wardrobe. The chap that lived here must have been similar in build to me.

                    YURI
The trousers are not a bad fit. A little short perhaps, but better than that charity stuff you got from the clothes bin.

                    DMITRY
Anything is better than that stuff.

          (Yuri takes another drink of coffee and Dmitry returns to his letter.)

                    YURI
What are you doing at desk? Have you come up with plan?

                    DMITRY
I have, well sort of.

                    YURI
Tell me.

          (Dmitry twists round to face Yuri.)

                    DMITRY
I am writing letter to News Station

explaining our story. I will put
camera card inside envelope with
letter and post it. This way,
someone will open it and hopefully be
intrigued enough to watch card. We
tried phoning and first contact, now
we will try old fashioned letter.

                    YURI
That is a good idea, but make sure
you put enough stamps on the envelope
or it will just stay at post office
for week and be thrown.

                  DMITRY
I have already put five first class
stamps on envelope and addressed it.

                    YURI
Seems like you have everything under
control.

                  DMITRY
We can creep out at first light
tomorrow and post it. If we just
hold up here for a few days relaxing
instead of running about like fools,
things might just work themselves
out.

                    YURI
Sitting about and relaxing. Sounds
perfect, almost too perfect...

*(Yuri takes another sip of
coffee and then puffs his
cigarette.)*

...I can't believe this thing is
nearly over. It will be good to get
back to our old lives. I think I
will go and have a shower and then
rake through the owner's wardrobe
myself.

                    DMITRY
Yes, better get it now while the
water is still hot.

                    YURI
See you in a while.

*(Yuri walks out of the room
towards the bathroom and
Dmitry finishes his letter.)*

Scene fades.

ACT 2, SCENE 6

9.37am. Saturday 15th February 1986, Moshennik House, Tiver, Russia. Inside, Colonel P. Chekov is putting on his tie in his study. His wife, Ruth, is in the hall arranging some daffodils in a vase that sits on a table. They are engaged in conversation.

> RUTH
You are going out again, I thought we were looking for a delivery truck this morning?

> COLONEL P. CHEKOV
I don't know if the poultry business is right for us just now.

> RUTH
We need to do something...

> *(Ruth runs her hands through the daffodils.)*

...We can't live on a Corporal's wage.

> COLONEL P. CHEKOV
I am not a Corporal yet...

> *(Colonel P. Chekov takes his tie off. He walks over to a*

*mirror in the room and starts
again.)*

...I told you, the hearing isn't
until next month, I just need to get
something on Spuriovsky before then.
Something juicy.

*(Ruth walks over to a coat
rack where her husband's
overcoat is hanging. She
rifles through his pockets,
takes some money out of his
wallet and tucks it in her
brassiere.)*

                    RUTH
It is your dirty dealings and your
scheming that got you into trouble in
the first place.

          COLONEL P. CHEKOV
I am not the one who wants to buy a
truck so we can steal chickens to
sell.

                    RUTH
Pah! If you were still a General we
wouldn't have to.

          COLONEL P. CHEKOV
Why can't you be a bit more
supportive towards me, like your
sister is to Melor?

                    RUTH
I have told her time and time again
she is too soft on her husband.
Melor will think he is loved.

              COLONEL P. CHEKOV
Would that be such a bad thing?

                    RUTH
Love is the ruin of a good man, it
makes him weak.

              COLONEL P. CHEKOV
That's what must of happened to me.
Your love has made me decrepit...

       (The Colonel is still
       struggling with his tie.)

...Aarrghh! Stupid thing, it's
impossible.

                    RUTH
What is wrong now?...

       (Ruth walks into the study
       where the Colonel is fighting
       with his tie.)

...Here, let me do it...

       (Ruth walks over to the
       Colonel and puts his tie on.)

...There, all done.

*(The Colonel looks in the
mirror.)*

COLONEL P. CHEKOV
Good. Thank you. Have you seen my
cufflinks and tie pin?

*(The Colonel walks over to
his desk and begins opening
drawers.)*

RUTH
I sold them.

(He looks up at his wife.)

COLONEL P. CHEKOV
You sold them. Why?

RUTH
I needed the money to buy the truck.

COLONEL P. CHEKOV
They were given to me by the
President himself.

RUTH
I know. I got a good price.

COLONEL P. CHEKOV
What am I supposed to do now?

                    RUTH
You have plenty more cufflinks in
that drawer of yours.

          (*The Colonel looks through
          his drawer and pulls out a
          triangular gold watch, some
          silver cufflinks and a gold
          bracelet.*)

          COLONEL P. CHEKOV
There was a strange looking gold ring
in this drawer, where is it?

                    RUTH
The one with a big red stone.

          COLONEL P. CHEKOV
That's it.

                    RUTH
I sold that as well.

          COLONEL P. CHEKOV
I hope you gave a false name at the
pawnbrokers.

                    RUTH
Why?

          COLONEL P. CHEKOV
That ring could land us in hot water
if it is traced back to us...

*(The Colonel picks up a pair
of cufflinks and puts them
on.)*

...I must have a tie pin.

                    RUTH
Why, what good is it?

              COLONEL P. CHEKOV
It stops the tie from hitting you in
the face when the wind blows.

                    RUTH
That is maybe not such a bad thing,
it might wake you up.

              COLONEL P. CHEKOV
Get me my shoes, I am running late.

                    RUTH
Get them yourself, I am not your
slave.

              COLONEL P. CHEKOV
I should have married your sister,
she is plain and stupid. I didn't
realise that they were attributes
when I was young.

                    RUTH
Well now you do. If you marry a

woman with a brain, you better have
your act together...

(Ruth hands her husband his
shoes.)

...Here. Here are your shoes. I can
see you are getting flustered my
little Yabloko and we don't want you
blowing a gasket.

                COLONEL P. CHEKOV
Thank you...

(The Colonel puts on his
shoes and gathers the
jewellery from the desk and
slides it in the draw. The
triangular watch falls on the
floor and a 'V' shaped
attachment detaches from the
back. It is gold with an
amethyst stone at the top
with alien writing on it.
The attachment appears to
contain several gears and
springs. The Colonel studies
it and smiles.)

...This is perfect. This will make
an excellent tie pin.

(The Colonel takes the watch
part, pierces his tie with it
and bends over the ends. He

throws the watch back in the
drawer.)

RUTH
Perhaps when you get back we can talk
about Spuriovsky and come up with a
plan.

COLONEL P. CHEKOV
Now we are talking. I am glad you
are on board. You have a knack for
the nefarious that I haven't quite
mastered yet and your help is always
welcome. Your devious side reminds
me why I love you so much.

(The doorbell rings.)

RUTH
Are you expecting anyone?

COLONEL P. CHEKOV
No, I am going out.

(Ruth peeks out the window.)

RUTH
It is General Spuriovsky.

COLONEL P. CHEKOV
What does he want?

                    RUTH
How should I know?

              COLONEL P. CHEKOV
You better show him in...

     (Ruth answers the door and
     shows the General into the
     study.)

...General, what a pleasant surprise.
I'm afraid you have caught me at an
inopportune time, I am just on my way
out.

              GENERAL SPURIOVSKY
Yes, I know. You are going to the
Tiver Museum for the coal exhibition.

              COLONEL P. CHEKOV
They have asked me to cut the ribbon
and make a speech.

              GENERAL SPURIOVSKY
So I understand. I have my car
outside waiting. We can ride there
together. I have something very
important I wish to speak to you
about and we can do that on the way.

     (The Colonel looks at his
     wife for a moment and then
     around the room.)

                    COLONEL P. CHEKOV
Yes, well alright.   I'll just cancel
my taxi.

Scene fades.

ACT 2, SCENE 7

On planet EgÁs, the afternoon brings
a cooler temperature and the extreme
heat of the midday sun has past. At
the foot of Ra-eb's Claw, Sir Gorf
Daot, Tac and Eeb look on in
bewilderment at the treasures that
lie within the exposed cave.
Advanced machinery, flying machines
and an arsenal of weaponry spread out
into the distance of a great
underground complex. Paintings,
statues, books, electronic equipment,
radar dishes, computers, house
furnishings stacked high on shelves
and an assortment of gold coins and
precious stones spill out across the
floor. At the cave entrance, a
multitude of EgÁsian hieroglyphs
cover the walls telling the stories
of long ago. Around the entrance,
fallen rocks, Sandweed and debris lay
scattered on a luminous bright blue
floor. Sir Gorf Daot, Tac, and Eeb
enter the cave cautiously.

SIR GORF DAOT
This is absolutely intoxicating,
don't know where to look first!

(Eeb picks up a gold coin.)

EEB
There's a date on this coin, but it

doesn't make any sense.

                    TAC
Look at all these hieroglyphs, there
is a lifetime's work here in study
alone, perhaps two lifetimes...

         (They all walk in a bit
         further.)

...Look at this Sir Daot!

               SIR GORF DAOT
What is it?

                    TAC
Well, it's absolutely fascinating.
It's the story about a mechanical
race of people who lived on EgÁs long
ago...

         (Tac points at a hieroglyph
         with some white figures.)

...It says here, if I am reading it
right. - IN THE YEAR 528KK,
ARTIFICIAL LIFE FORMS, KNOWN AS THE
DRELP, WERE CREATED TO PERFORM
DANGEROUS TASKS IN ÁDEL and COLÁ
MINES...

         (Tac runs his hand along the
         wall and cleans some dirt
         away. Eeb walks over to look

at the hieroglyphs.)

...This next bit is broken, but then it says - AFTER THE DEATH OF KING KÁNTDIE AND THE GREAT COUNCIL OF ARKANAZAK FROM POISONING, THE PEOPLE OF EGÁS ROSE UP AGAINST THE DRELP AND BLAMED THEM FOR THE CRIME...

(Tac points at a white figure on the wall.)

...If you look here, you can see the life forms are depicted as being white in colour.

　　　　　　SIR GORF DAOT
Yes, a real pale face. As white as flour I would say. What else does it say?

　　　　　　　　TAC
It would appear that after a long war fighting the Drelp, the ancient EgÁsians were nearly wiped out. As a result, they turned their backs on the technology that nearly destroyed them and buried it in this chamber...

(Tac turns to face Sir Gorf Daot. Eeb walks closer to study the hieroglyphs.)

...There's obviously a whole lot more to the story, but that's the gist of the thing.

                    EEB
Are you sure that's what it's saying?

                    TAC
More or less. Why?

                    TAC
Well, if you look at these three
fellows here...

          (Sir Daot and Tac look at the
          hieroglyphs.)

...The ones holding onto a big bag
and walking out of a bakery.

              SIR GORF DAOT
Yes, I see them, but how do you know
it's a bakery?

                    EEB
Well, if you look close, you can see
what looks like different types of
bread on display.

              SIR GORF DAOT
Oh, yes. He's right Tac.

                    TAC
I hardly think so, sir.

SIR GORF DAOT
Go on Eeb, you were saying...

EEB
Well, in this next picture, the three
men have no bag and the man next to
them is white. I reckon they threw a
bag of flour over that poor fellow as
a complaint.

SIR GORF DAOT
A complaint?

EEB
Well, yes...

*(Eeb points at another
glyph.)*

...If you look at this earlier
picture, the same three men have a
bakery with no bread. The flour must
have been of poor quality and
unusable. As a retribution, they
went back to the chap who sold it to
them and threw it in his face.

SIR GORF DAOT
Byjove, Eeb! I think you've cracked
this glyph lark, what do you say Tac?

TAC
It's absolute nonsense. I've never

heard so much rubbish. Three men and a bakery!...

(Tac becomes agitated and
points at a glyph.)

...This section here refers to a
hundred years of war, not to the
transference of flour from one
location to another.

                    EEB
Well, it's all open to
interpretation, boyo.

               SIR GIRF DAOT
He's right Tac,

                    TAC
What are you saying Sir Daot? That
you would take the misguided
gibberish of a lowly SelÁw tribesman
over a scholar with 15 years of
experience in the deciphering of
ancient EgÁsian hieroglyphs.

                    EEB
Less of the lowly SelÁw tribesman, if
you don't mind. If it wasn't for
Nelson and MacTavish, you would have
never found this place. You'd still
be wandering around in circles
pretending to know what you're doing.

                    SIR GORF DAOT
He's right Tac.

                         TAC
I can't believe you are siding with
Eeb.

                         EEB
Hang on, that reminds me, have you
seen MacTavish since the cave in?

                    SIR GORF DAOT
I haven't, have you Tac?

                         TAC
No, the last time I saw him was in
King KÁnTdiE's tomb. The last thing
we knew, he was coming back to the
surface to get some food. He left
before we did. We were the last
one's out.

                         EEB
Well, he never came back up.

                    SIR GORF DAOT
Maybe he got lost in a different
tunnel.

                         TAC
Maybe, couldn't say. Well, there's
no getting him out now.

*(They walk outside and look
towards a big hole in the
sand where the ground has
collapsed.)*

EEB

Poor old MacTavish.

TAC

Sorry, Eeb. I know MacTavish was a
good friend of yours. We'll have a
ceremony tonight in his honour.

*(From the direction of the
camp, Nelson and EffÁrig walk
over to Sir Daot, Tac and
Eeb.)*

NELSON

Has anyone see MacTavish?

EEB

No, we've just realised he never
returned from the Tomb of King
KÁnTdiE.

NELSON

Oh, that is bad news.

TAC

I was just telling Eeb we would have
a bit of a ceremony tonight in his
honour.

                    NELSON
That'll be nice. A bit of a booze up
like?

                  SIR GORF DAOT
I don't know about a booze up Nelson,
more of a toast.

                    NELSON
Oh, I see. Anyway, I've got some
more bad news.

                    TAC
More bad news?

                    NELSON
Well, you know how you sent me up top
to stop EffÁrig from going into town?

                    TAC
Yes?

                    NELSON
Well I did that alright, but he
forgot to tell me he sent someone
else in his place on account of his
bad foot.

                    TAC
What?

        (Nelson looks at EffÁrig.)

                    NELSON
I'll let the boy tell you.

                    EFFÁRIG
Well, it's like this. My foot was
giving me trouble and my friend Árbez
was hungry.

                    TAC
Is that it?

                    EFFÁRIG
More or less.

                    TAC
Nelson, what's EffÁrig trying to say?

                    NELSON
He gave his friend, Árbez, Sir Daot's
telegram to take into town. In
return, he would give Árbez the slice
of meat Sir Daot promised him.

                    TAC
How long ago was this?

                    NELSON
Hours ago. I would imagine Árbez is
in the city by now.

                    TAC
This is terrible, by this time
tomorrow this whole place will be a

circus. Reporters, photographers,
looters; this is a disaster. What if
the Yangolites hear about this?

NELSON

Not to mention the Zilotacs, they are
the worst of the lot. Wouldn't want
to be around if they turn up.

TAC

Absolutely not. Those Zilotacs are a
psychotic bunch. Riding about on
hortles as if they owned the place
and burning down villages and killing
hefolkans because they didn't believe
in the teachings of ZED. It's an
utter disgrace.

NELSON

I remember they burned down an entire
village belonging to the HA-V-OHE,
just because they had a statue of HUE
in the Square and not ZED.

SIR GORF DAOT

Oh dear, what are we to do?

EEB

I reckon we take what we can and
leave. Quit while the going's good
like.

SIR GORF DAOT
What, and leave all of this behind?

EEB
It's better than waiting around for
the Yangolites or the Zilotacs to
turn up. The whole place will be a
bloodbath!

SIR GORF DAOT
Oh, dear. Can't help but think this
is my fault. What shall we do Tac?

TAC
Let me think a minute.

Scene fades.

ACT 2, SCENE 8

7.17pm. Saturday 18th October 2025, Lengrasky railway station, Moscow. The train leaving for Tiver still sits in the station. The conductor is now taking tickets and enters the compartment next to London and his group of ex-SAS soldiers. Through the partition, they can hear a disturbance between some men and the conductor. A short while later, the door slides open to their compartment and the conductor walks in.

> TRAIN CONDUCTOR
Bilety, pozhaluysta?

> WINSLOW
He wants our tickets.

> LONDON
Yes, I think we all know that Winslow.

> *(The conductor holds out a ticket punch in his hand.)*

> TRAIN CONDUCTOR
Aah, you are English?

                    LONDON
Yes.

                TRAIN CONDUCTOR
Big Ben. Strawberries and Cream.
Buckingham Palace.

        (The conductor takes their
        tickets and begins to punch
        them.)

                    LONDON
Quite.

                TRAIN CONDUCTOR
My English is good, no?

                    LONDON
Yes, very good...

        (London takes his ticket
        back.)

...Sounds like you had a bit of
trouble next door?

                TRAIN CONDUCTOR
Trouble? No. Just someone trying to
get a free ride.

        (The conductor hands back the
        other tickets.)

LONDON
A free ride?

TRAIN CONDUCTOR
Yes. The man next door claimed his
overcoat had been stolen in the
Gent's toilets and his ticket was
inside. There are three of them in
the carriage. They all seemed most
upset over some tickets to a Tea
Convention they were going to
tomorrow in Tiver and that they will
have to pay again.

LONDON
Stolen overcoat you say?

TRAIN CONDUCTOR
Yes, but it is probably a scam.
People are always trying to get a
free ride.

LONDON
Yes. Better than paying.

(They all laugh along with
the conductor.)

TRAIN CONDUCTOR
I see you are going to Tiver. There
is going to be a delay of 20 minutes.

                    CAVENDISH
Why is that?

                    TRAIN CONDUCTOR
Some terrible business with a
military train on the other track.
The signalman got drunk and the
points didn't get changed.

                    CAVENDISH
Was anybody hurt?

                    TRAIN CONDUCTOR
A few, but nothing major. The train
is off the track and the engine is
ruined so they are transferring the
soldiers onto this train to meet up
with a transport in Okshin.

                    LONDON
What about the signalman?

                    TRAIN CONDUCTOR
They shot him.

                    LONDON
Shot him? Yes, well thank you.

                    TRAIN CONDUCTOR
Have a good trip, gentlemen.

          *(The door slides closed and
          the conductor moves on to the*

next compartment.)

                    LONDON
Pity about that signalman. Seemed a
decent sort.

                  PILKINGTON
What are we going to do now? The
train is going to be full of Russian
soldiers.

                    LONDON
Best to keep a calm head in these
situations Pilky. We don't want to
panic, panic is the ticket to
ruination. We'll just play it out.

                  CAVENDISH
Play it out?

                    LONDON
Yes. I don't see the need to be
concerned about this. They are
getting off at Okshin. We will just
stay in here out of their way. We
are just six men on holiday. They
have already found the perpetrator of
that train crash, so we are in the
clear. If I was you, I would take
this opportunity to get some rest.
We won't be bothered if we appear
asleep.

                    CARTWRIGHT
London's right, and a sleep sounds
good.

                     CARTER
I think I'll keep one eye open all
the same.

     (Outside, the snow picks up
     again and the wind whistles
     through the station. London
     and his men snuggle down and
     rest their eyes.)

Scene fades.

ACT 2, SCENE 9

7.31pm. Saturday 18th October 2025,
'The Dragon's Breath' public house,
Flat 1A, Moscow. Dmitry and Yuri are
sitting on the couch playing a game of
Cribbage. Yuri is 15 points ahead and
only 30 points away from 'pegging-
out'. The score is being kept on an
official wooden board - It's Yuri's
turn to go.

                    YURI
Queen of Spades, for thirty.

          (Yuri places the card on the
          table.)

                    DMITRY

I can't go.

                    YURI
For one...

          (Yuri moves his peg one step
          closer to the finish.)

...My first count. Fifteen two,
fifteen four and a pair is six.

                    DMITRY
Six points, not bad, but I have
eight...

*(Dmitry lays his cards on the
table.)*

...And look, another 4 in the box.

YURI
You need them, you are behind...

*(Dmitry deals out a new hand.
They pick up the cards and
begin to sort them.)*

...I am glad to be clean again and
just relaxing.

DMITRY
Yes, it is nice to be out of trouble
for five minutes.

YURI
You are telling me. Do you think it
will soon be over?

DMITRY
Almost. General Gerasimov is dead.
That stupid goblin woman is dead.
Kantcoughsky is dead. That Vadim guy
is dead. We are cutting them down.
Now if we can take out the kingpin in
this mess, we will be in the clear.

YURI
You mean that Spuriovsky chap?

Another rotten egg. I can't believe
he has given orders for our capture
on the pretext we are goblins.

                    DMITRY
Yes, it is a shame we ever met that
Decapinovsky woman. She has
propagated a rumour that has only
added to our problem...

     (Dmitry cuts the pack.)

...Turn the card over.

     *(Yuri turns over the card and
     places it on top of the
     pack.)*

                    YURI
A Jack.

                    DMITRY
I get *'two for his heels'*.

                    YURI
Lucky start.

     *(Yuri lays the 9 of clubs.
     Dmitry looks through his hand
     and lays the 6 of diamonds.)*

                    DMITRY
Fifteen for two...

(*Yuri adds the score to the
board.*)

...I can tell you one thing.

                    YURI
What is that?

                    DMITRY
I am glad we don't have that
Medallion of Life trinket. It seems
to be at the bottom of everything and
the route of our current dilemma.
Even the aliens want it. I am glad
that loud mouthed English chap has
it.

                    YURI
Are you not a bit curious about it?

                    DMITRY
No. When a lot of people want the
same thing as badly as that, you will
never be free of trouble.

                    YURI
But it must be important. Have some
sort of power.

                    DMITRY
Maybe so, but it is better left
alone. I have seen greed and envy
before. Death always follows.

                    YURI
Oh!... Ten of Diamonds - Twenty
five. You need six or less to go.

                    DMITRY
What is Oh?

                    YURI
Eh?

                    DMITRY
You said Oh! And then placed a card
down...

        *(Dmitry lays down a 4 of
        spades.)*

...Is there something you are not
telling me?

                    YURI
Not really.

                    DMITRY
What does that mean?

                    YURI
I have the Medallion.

                    DMITRY
You have it, how?

                    YURI
I took it from that Carter fellow
when he was next to the white alien.

                  DMITRY
Why would you do that?

                    YURI
I thought it might come in handy.

        (Dmitry gets to his feet,
        picks up a bottle of Vodka
        and pours a drink. Yuri
        lights a cigarette.)

                  DMITRY
And what do you think will happen
when the English find out they don't
have it anymore?

                    YURI
I didn't think of that. I just
thought it was important that is
all...

        (Yuri takes a puff from his
        cigarette.)

...besides, I can't imagine the
English will come looking for it.
They will have their own troubles.

                  DMITRY
Where is it now?

                        YURI
It is in my pocket. Why?

                       DMITRY
Let me see it.

          (Yuri hands Dmitry the
          Medallion. Dmitry holds it
          in his hands a moment than
          passes it back to Yuri.)

                        YURI
It is very pretty and quite heavy.
Must be worth a few thousand Rubles.

                       DMITRY
I imagine so. Just get ready to
throw it if we get caught again.
It's probably best destroyed.

                        YURI
Without knowing what it is?

                       DMITRY
Some things are better left unknown.

                        YURI
You sound just like my mother when I
would question her about my father.

          (Dmitry pours another drink
          then looks at Yuri.)

>   DMITRY
> How did you get it off that Carter
> chap without him noticing?

>   YURI
> I am a good pickpocket. The secret
> is to replace a heavy item with
> something of similar weight.

>   DMITRY
> Sounds logical. What did you use?

>   YURI
> A tin of tuna.

>   DMITRY
> A tin of tuna?...

>   *(Dmitry starts to laugh.)*

> ...I would have loved to have seen
> that stupid Carter fellow's face when
> he pulled out a tin of tuna instead
> of Medallion.

>   *(Yuri starts to smile.)*

>   YURI
> I would imagine he was pretty upset.

>   *(They both begin to laugh.*
>   *Dmitry takes his seat again.)*

                    DMITRY
So, you are a pickpocket as well?

                     YURI
It is a family tradition.

                    DMITRY
What do you mean?

                     YURI
Our family have been pickpockets for
years, in fact, it was my great,
great, great uncle Si who first
turned it into a trade.

                    DMITRY
I would hardly call pickpocketing a
trade. It is your turn.

        (Yuri throws down the two of
        hearts.)

                     YURI
Thirty one for two...

        (Yuri moves his peg two
        points.)

...My, great, great, great uncle Si
even had a partner to do the work for
him.

DMITRY
A partner?

YURI
Yes, he had a little Capuchin monkey
to work crowd while he put on show.

(Dmitry starts to laugh.)

DMITRY
What rubbish you speak Yuri. A
monkey to work crowd! What kind of
show was it?

YURI
A travelling Flea Circus.

DMITRY
A Flea Circus?

YURI
Yes, I believe it was quite something
to behold. As my father tells it,
there were miniature chariot races,
blindfolded tightrope walkers,
unicycle riders and freestyle diving
board jumpers. Obviously it wasn't
real and there were no fleas, but a
clever clockwork mechanism of gears
and pulleys made it look so. To the
untrained eye, the whole show was
believable.

(Yuri lights a cigarette and

sits back.)

> DMITRY
> As always Yuri, you have managed to
> tell me nothing.

> YURI
> What do you mean?

> DMITRY
> You have left out the part about pick
> pocketing.

> YURI
> Did I?...

> *(Dmitry places the five of*
> *clubs on the table.)*

...Oh, yes. While audience was
captivated with Flea show. Si's
partner, the Capuchin monkey, would
jump in amongst the crowd and lift
wallets, rings, necklaces, watches,
snuff boxes and anything else he
could find. He would then return to
Si and hide everything in his wooden
leg...

> *(Yuri lays the Jack of*
> *Diamonds.)*

...Ha! Fifteen for two.

(Yuri moves his peg.)

DMITRY
His wooden leg?

YURI
Yes, Si had a wooden leg.

*(Dmitry throws down his last
card, the 4 of hearts.)*

DMITRY
That's nineteen for one... Did he
lose it in the Caucasian war?

*(Dmitry lays down the four of
Diamonds.)*

YURI
No, he jumped out of barn from top
floor and landed on plough.

DMITRY
Was it for a dare?

YURI
No. Farmer return home early from
work to fix broken wagon wheel. In
barn, where he keep tools, he find Si
engaged in amorous congress with
wife.

                    DMITRY
Your great, great, great uncle Si was
a rogue.

                    YURI
Maybe, but he did redeem himself.
Him and his monkey.

                    DMITRY
How?

                    YURI
He joined Imperial Army and fought at
Russian Conquest of Asia.

                    DMITRY
The Russian Conquest of Asia?

                    YURI
Yes, him and his monkey.

                    DMITRY
This is ridiculous Yuri, he had a
wooden leg.

                    YURI
Even so, he was awarded the *Dauntless
Medal of the Undismayed*.

                    DMITRY
I have never heard of it.

                        YURI
It is a very rare award.

                        DMITRY
What does it look like?

                        YURI
It is a gold triangle with a fist in
the centre holding a sprig of
chamomile...

          *(Yuri begins counting his
          cards.)*

...My father has it on display along
with my great, great, great uncle
Si's portrait.

                        DMITRY
What happened to the monkey?

                        YURI
He was promoted to rank of Captain.

                        DMITRY
Captain? This is tale of distraction
while you win game. How can a monkey
become a Captain in Imperial Army?

                        YURI
Well it is truth, take it or leave
it.

DMITRY

Aarrggh. It is my first count up...

*(Dmitry lays his cards down
and begins to count the
score.)*

...Fifteen two, fifteen four, fifteen
six, a pair is eight and a run of
4,5,6 twice equals 14 points. I am
catching up.

YURI

Yes, it is my turn now and I have the
box...

*(Yuri lays his cards on the
table.)*

...No fifteens... A pair of Jacks for
two, plus nine, ten, Jack in a run
twice. For a total of 8 points. I
need eleven for game...

*(Yuri turns over the 'box'
cards, The 3 of clubs, 3 of
spades, 2 of diamonds and the
9 of hearts.)*

...Fifteen two, fifteen four, fifteen
six and a pair for a total of 8
points. I just need 3 points for
game.

                    DMITRY
How many do I need?

                    YURI
12.

                    DMITRY
It is close, but you get first count
this time.

                    YURI
I would say it is over Dmitry.

                    DMITRY
We will see. Never say die.

                    YURI
Even in the face of insurmountable
odds and absolutely no chance of
success you play on.

                    DMITRY
What else can I do? Don't tell me
it's over until it's over. Only when
I have lost, I will admit defeat.

          (Dmitry shuffles the cards
          and deals them out, Yuri
          looks at his cards.)

                    YURI
You might be in with a chance, I have

rubbish. It depends what the turn up card is.

> *(The turn up card is selected, the 2 of Spades.)*

DMITRY

Your move.

YURI

I have nothing, and that turn up card was tripe!

> *(Yuri lays the two of Diamonds.)*

DMITRY

A low card, you must be in trouble...

> *(Dmitry lays the 3 of Diamonds.)*

...There, I have given you a chance.

YURI

If I had a 10, it would have been good...

> *(Yuri places the 6 of clubs on the table and Dmitry throws down the 5 of Spades.)*

Here, have an Ace.

(Yuri throws down the Ace of spades, Dmitry studies his hand.)

DMITRY
Ha! I have a run...

(Dmitry throws down the 4 of hearts.)

...For six points. Beat that.

YURI
I can't believe it.

(Yuri moves Dmitry's peg and they lay their final cards - The 3 of Spades and the 7 of Diamonds. Dmitry wins another point.)

DMITRY
I only need 5 points.

YURI
Yes, but it is over. My first count...

(Yuri scans his cards.)

...I have 8. I win. Now pay up?

DMITRY
I didn't hear the stake, what was it?

                    YURI
To sacrifice your life for mine.

                   DMITRY
What?

                    YURI
If we are in trouble and the lead
starts to fly, I want you to jump in
front of me and take bullet.

                   DMITRY
Perhaps I should have read the rules
to this game before we played. That
part must have been in the fine
print.

     (They both laugh.)

Scene fades.

ACT 2, SCENE 10

8.32pm. Saturday 18th October 2025,
Avidov railway station, Russia. A
group of passengers board the train
and take a seat where they can. Two
of the main carriages are full of
Russian soldiers and the train is
nearly full. An elderly couple walk
through the train and enter London and
his group of ex-SAS soldier's
compartment. The man places some
luggage on a rack above the seats and
Carter and Cartwright move over to
give them room to sit. The man and
the woman sit down opposite one
another and smile. London and the
others begin to stir after a short
sleep.

London
Where are we Cavendish?

> (Cavendish rolls his eyes in
> the direction of the elderly
> couple to tell London they
> are not alone. London wipes
> his eyes, then looks at the
> couple.)

CAVENDISH
We are at Avidov station.

LONDON
Ah, good. Won't be long now.

WINSLOW
Do you think there's a toilet on the
train?

LONDON
You can't possibly want to go again.

WINSLOW
I've got a chill. It's gone right
through me.

LONDON
Can't you wait until we get to Tiver?

WINSLOW
No.

*(The elderly couple begin
speaking and laughing in
Russian. London looks over
to the woman.)*

LONDON
I understand some Russian y'know. My
friend has a weak bladder, it's
nothing to laugh about.

OLD WOMAN
It is funny that the old man asks you
for toilet. Is he your father?

LONDON
No, my uncle.

*(The old woman looks at
London and his gang.)*

OLD WOMAN
You are a strange looking bunch.
What brings you to Russia?

LONDON
We were here for the festival.

OLD WOMAN
So your friend has had too much to
drink?

LONDON
Well, you know what it's like, boys
together and all that.

OLD WOMAN
They say men never grow up, now I see
it is true.

LONDON
You have quite an acid tongue for a
small woman.

(The husband is smiling.)

OLD MAN
You have heard nothing yet.

*(The old woman turns to her
husband.)*

OLD WOMAN
Be quiet and read your paper.

*(The old man stops smiling
and takes out the evening
newspaper from his pocket.
He unfolds it and begins to
read the 'looking for love'
column in the personals
section.)*

WINSLOW
It's no good, I'll have to go.

*(Winslow gets up from his
seat and brushes past the old
man reading his newspaper.
Carter notices the headline
on the front page - 'ALIEN
INVASION DESTROYS AUTUMN
DRINKS FESTIVAL'. Underneath
the headline is a big picture
of the 'Red Neval' on fire
with Dmitry, Yuri, MacTavish,
KAL, London and his group of
ex-SAS soldiers emerging from
the wreck. A blow up of
their faces appears as a
strip along the bottom of the
newspaper with the tag:
'WANTED - CONSIDERED*

EXTREMELY DANGEROUS'.)

                    LONDON
Don't talk to anyone and come
straight back.

    (Carter nudges Pilkington's
    elbow to look at the
    newspaper, and a nudging game
    starts until all but the old
    man and woman have examined
    the front page of the
    newspaper.)

                  OLD WOMAN
You have no respect for your uncle,
he is not a dog.

                    LONDON
Oh, I see. Well, erm, it's not like
that. He has a tendency to get
involved with strangers. If someone
offers him a boiled sweet he could be
lost for days.

                  OLD WOMAN
You will be old one day, then you
will realise what you have done.

    (Outside in the corridor,
    Winslow is engaged in a
    heated argument with the man
    from the next compartment.

The conductor comes to see
the disturbance. Some
Russian soldiers look on from
the carriage.)

RUSSIAN MAN
U tebya yest' moye pal'to!

WINSLOW
Get off me, want do you want?

RUSSIAN MAN
Vy ukrali moye pal'to. Day eto mne.

(The conductor enters the
foray.)

WINSLOW
Get this man off me.

(The conductor and the
Russian man speak for a
moment.)

CONDUCTOR
This man says you have his coat...

(The Russian man pulls at the
coat.)

...He says his name is stitched
inside.

(*The conductor looks at a*
name tag inside the coat.)

...Is your name Viktor Pokrovsky?

                    WINSLOW
No.

(*The Russian man speaks*
again.)

                    CONDUCTOR
He wants you to turn out the pockets.
He says there will be a first class
ticket to Tiver and 3 tickets to the
Annual Tea Convention, also in Tiver.
Now, please empty your pockets.

(*After a few moments, Winslow*
reluctantly empties his
pockets and displays the
items in question.)

                    CONDUCTOR
Stay there, this is a police matter
now.

(*As the conductor walks away*
he is stopped by a captain
from the Russian platoon on
board the train.)

                    CAPTAIN
Mogu li ya byt' poleznym?...

*(The captain and the
Conductor speak for a moment
and then he walks over to
Winslow.)*

...You are English?

*(The Russian man starts
pulling at his overcoat and
begins to make a scene.
London and Carter go out into
the corridor to see what the
fuss is. London walks over
to Winslow.)*

LONDON
Ah, Winslow there you are. Come
along now, back to the compartment.

CAPTAIN
Do you know this man?

LONDON
Yes, he's my uncle.

CAPTAIN
He has stolen this man's overcoat.

*(London takes the overcoat
off of Winslow and hands it
back to the Russian man.)*

LONDON
Yes, well sorry about that. He gets
confused at times. He probably
picked up the wrong coat.

*(London, Winslow and Carter
go to walk back to their
compartment.)*

CAPTAIN
Just a minute. How many others are
in your party?

(London turns back around.)

LONDON
Three more, why?

CAPTAIN
We are looking for 6 Englishmen in
connection with a stolen handbag. Do
you know anything about that?

LONDON
A handbag! No, absolutely not.

CAPTAIN
Where have you been today?

LONDON
We were at the Vodka festival. Then
we came here.

CAPTAIN
I will need to see your passports.

LONDON
Why, we haven't done anything.

*(The Captain puts his hand on
his hip next to his
revolver.)*

CAPTAIN
I won't ask again.

*(Cavendish, Pilkington and
Cartwright listen to the
disturbance from the
compartment. The old woman
looks at the Newspaper's
front page, grabs it and runs
into the corridor shouting.)*

OLD WOMAN
Inoplanetyane, eto inoplanetyane!

*(Cavendish, Pilkington and
Cartwright grab the guns from
under the seats and enter the
corridor. They fire widely
at the ceiling and everyone
ducks.)*

CAVENDISH
C'mon, get out of there!

(Carter, London and Winslow run from the corridor back into the compartment. Cavendish continues to fire into the ceiling along with Cartwright and Pilkington. Shortly afterwards, they dive into their compartment.)

LONDON

Thanks Cavendish, you jumped in at the right moment there. That Captain fellow was getting an itchy trigger finger.

(Shots ring out into the corridor and ricochet off the floor. The old Russian man looks very frightened.)

LONDON

Stop firing! We have an old Russian man in here. He is very scared.

(Out in the corridor, Russian soldiers begin advancing on their position and aim their rifles at London's compartment. The Captain moves forward and shouts out.)

CAPTAIN

What are your demands?

                              LONDON
What do you mean?

                              CAPTAIN
For the release of your hostage.

          (London looks at his team.)

                              LONDON
I'm afraid you've misunderstood. We
just want you to stop firing so he
can join you without getting hurt.
If you wait a moment, we will send
him out.

          *(The Captain motions to his
          troops to lower their
          rifles.)*

                              CAPTAIN
Alright. We won't fire.

          *(London points to Cavendish
          to open the outside door to
          their compartment.)*

                              LONDON
Right, c'mon we are getting off this
train.

          *(Cavendish opens the door and
          the wind and the snow rush
          in.)*

CARTWRIGHT

I'm not going out there. Not with my
leg.

LONDON

Man up Cartwright. You've had plenty
of rest.

WINSLOW

What about me, I haven't got a coat.

LONDON

Take the old man's, he can get
another.

    (Winslow takes the old man's
    overcoat and puts it on.)

WINSLOW

Not bad, a much better fit than the
last one.

    (Cavendish sticks his head
    outside and looks down the
    track.)

CAVENDISH

If we're going, we better go now,
there's a bridge coming up.

LONDON

Right, Okay, everyone out. I'll stay
here with this fellow. You go first

Cavendish, then try and catch the
rest as they come out.

CAPTAIN
We are waiting.

LONDON
He is coming out now.

*(Cavendish, Cartwright,
Winslow, Pilkington and
Carter jump from the train
out into the snow and wind.
Moments later, London jumps
out leaving the old man in
the compartment.)*

CAPTAIN
We are still waiting.

*(The train continues to speed
down the track and crosses a
Truss bridge over the Okshin
river and disappears out of
sight.)*

Scene fades.

End of Part I

FIND OUT WHAT HAPPENS NEXT IN:

UPRISING · PART II

If you have time, please rate and leave a review on Amazon to help increase awareness of this series. Many thanks, Sam Lucas.

To see the complete collection of books in this series, please go to: **www.samlucasbooks.com**